Murder at the Front

A 1920s historical mystery prequel

A Dora and Rex Mystery

Lynn Morrison

Cover design by DLR Cover Designs

Paperback ISBN: 978-1-7392632-5-6

Published by

The Marketing Chair Press, Oxford, England

LynnMorrisonWriter.com

Contents

To Inga - You'll live forever on the page

Chapter 1
A Most Unlikely Marriage

Given she'd sworn to never marry, Lady Dorothy's wedding day was turning out to be surprisingly enjoyable.

She tucked the precious bottle of 1914 Pol Roger and the accompanying tin box tight against her chest and jerked her head in time to avoid it being bashed against the peeling paint on the wooden doorframe. Her new husband stumbled through and kicked the door shut behind them before dropping her unceremoniously onto the bed.

"Now you've done it," she chastised, although there was no heat behind her words. "We'll be lucky if the bottle doesn't explode before you get it open."

Her husband Lucien held out a hand in a silent request. After she relinquished her hold on the bottle, he crossed the room, shoved aside the curtain, and opened the window. With a quick twist of his hand, he sent the cork flying into the darkness outside with a laugh of delight and a cheer from below.

Lady Dorothy Cavendish, or Dora as she was known to friends, grabbed two chipped mugs from the small table and hurried to his side. "Don't waste it, Lucien! It will be the last bottle either of us is likely to see for months."

Lucien, however, was in full control of his actions. He poured with a deft hand, shifting the bottle upright in time to keep a single drop from spilling over onto the worn wooden floor. He set the bottle on top of the mantle and raised his mug in a toast.

"To the woman who swore she'd never marry," he said, eyeing her with a smile.

"To the man who said the same," she replied, without missing a beat. She tossed back the contents of her mug and held it out for a refill.

"Touché, old girl. We're quite a pair, aren't we?"

"A match made in heaven, I believe, is what the priest said."

"More like one made on the battlefield," Lucien corrected. "I'm hard pressed to say which one of us comes out better in this arrangement."

Dora slipped out of her heels, sighing in relief as she rubbed the red mark they'd worn on the side of her foot. That was the problem with borrowed shoes. She took another sip of her champagne as she weighed Lucien's question. He'd meant it to be rhetorical, but she couldn't stop herself from answering.

"That's simple. It's your sister."

Lucien choked on his champagne, making Dora giggle. "Ahh, yes. Genevieve will be beside herself once she hears the news. She's been dreaming of you joining our family since the day you first set foot in the dormitories of Saint Bernadette's. Although, I daresay this isn't exactly what she had in mind."

"No, I think not." Dora gave Lucien a wry smile. "Her visions included cherubic nieces and nephews with my blonde curls and your blue eyes. Safe to say that isn't in the cards."

Lucien shook his head, his mouth wrinkling at the mere thought of it. He grabbed the bottle from the mantle and motioned for Dora to make space for him on the bed. She did as he asked, moving gingerly so as not to spill her drink. He topped his own glass and then set the bottle within reach.

The evening was quiet, or as quiet as it got in Le Touquet, a former seaside town turned wartime command post. Dora was grateful she wasn't living in the tents where the enlisted men slept down the road in Étaples. A decade earlier, the wealthy flocked to these shores for sun and a hint of freedom. Dora was sure none of them ever imagined their hotels and casinos would soon become officer quarters and hospitals.

Several years of housing officers and refugees had worn much of the shine off this particular hotel. Dora shifted around until she was leaning against the footboard, facing Lucien.

"At the rate this bloody war is progressing, it will be a long while before anyone will pressure us about children. We'll be lucky enough to survive with our limbs intact. Case in point, it's our wedding night and you're expected to leave tomorrow for another one of your missions."

"Needs must, old bean. For now, let's focus our attentions on this dreadful bottle of champagne and the box of chocolates Lord Audley gave us. About the only nice thing I can say about them both is they're better than our normal rations."

The pair toasted themselves again, both hardly able to believe they'd pulled it off. Dora glimpsed the two of them in the mirror hanging on the far wall. If she squinted, she could almost imagine she was back in the dormitory of the Swiss finishing school, hidden away with her best friend Genevieve.

They'd spent many an hour sitting in their room as punishment for one shenanigan or another. They could hardly be blamed. After all, being sent away to boarding school hadn't been either of their idea. But their parents had been determined to see them both polished and groomed before sending them onto the marriage mart.

Of course, they hadn't foreseen the start of the Great War and the death of so many eligible bachelors of their generation. Genevieve had retreated to her parents' home in France. Dorothy had ignored her summons, running off to join the war effort as a nurse. It took a full year of bloody bedside work to prove her mettle before her parents had accepted her decision.

She could hardly believe her luck when she ran into Genevieve's brother Lucien in Le Touquet. Tall, strong, with thick chestnut hair and a debonair style, Lucien was fit for the starring role in a debutante's dreams. Only she knew that his gaze was pulled elsewhere.

It was a secret she'd held tight until just the right moment. After her brother died in the second Battle of the Somme and the Germans bombed the Canadian hospitals in Le Touquet, Dora's father threatened to withhold her inheritance if she didn't come home to safety.

"You can tend to soldiers here, Dora," her mother had written. "My heart can't bear another loss."

It wasn't that Dorothy was completely unfeeling. The news of her brother's death had sent her to bed for a week. But only the knowledge of other young men bravely facing a similar fate had given her the wherewithal to carry on. He'd given everything. Could she offer any less?

She'd cornered Lucien with a proposal he couldn't refuse. He'd taken it better than she'd expected.

Dora untwisted her own blonde locks from their tight knot, letting them tumble over her shoulders and cover part of her face. Thus hidden, she dared to ask the question lingering in her mind. "Are you having second thoughts?"

"No... are you?"

"Definitely not... although, since we've pledged to keep no secrets from one another, I should admit I'm nervous about that telegram I sent to my mother. She'll be devastated that we didn't wait until war end so she could organise a lavish wedding. How will your parents react?"

"My mother will swoon, but more from shock than disappointment. I made my thoughts on the institution known many a time. She'll certainly wonder about the motivations behind my change of heart."

"I'm sure Genevieve will have no trouble listing my various accomplishments," Dorothy assured him.

Despite her saucy wink, Lucien didn't laugh. He reached over with his free hand and brushed her hair from her face, forcing her to meet his eyes. "You do know this is a terrible thing we've done—forcing the priest to marry us under false pretence, without telling either of our families."

War front ceremony or no, Dorothy refused to feel shame about her marriage of convenience. "No worse than many others. Take my own parents. Father needed money. Grandmother wanted a title in the family. That Father and Mother fell in love later was sheer happenstance. Most arranged marriages at that level don't end in happiness."

"That is true. My parents were second cousins." Lucien shivered in revulsion. "A little too close family, as far as I'm concerned."

"If the rumours about my mother's family are true, my second cousin robbed a bank in the American west. Successfully, I might add." Dorothy tossed back the last of her champagne and pretended to concentrate. "I hadn't given thought to that possibility. Maybe I have made a mistake. I could be living in the lap of luxury right now, relishing in his newfound wealth."

Lucien took the mug from her hand and leaned over to refill both their glasses from what little was left. He handed it back with a gentle suggestion to sip what was there.

"We both know a life without activity doesn't suit you,

you know me better than anyone else in this world. I couldn't bear the thought of anything happening to you."

Lucien tied his laces and stood, smoothing his uniform over his muscular torso. Only the tightness of his jaw betrayed his nerves. He took a deep breath and closed his eyes, working up his courage to leave the relative safety of their room. He leaned over and kissed Dorothy on the top of her head.

"Cheer up, Dorothy. You know what they say. *Only the good die young.* I certainly don't fit that bill. Besides, it's only a messenger mission. I won't even be near the trenches."

Dorothy kept her silence, not daring to correct his interpretation of that ancient Greek proverb, but she couldn't stop it from flashing through her head.

"Whom the gods love, dies young, Call no man blessed until he is dead."

Chapter 2
The Path Not Taken

It was a draft of warm night air that dragged Lord Reginald from his sleep. When he opened his eyes, all he saw was a dark shadow hovering above his face. A calloused hand covered his mouth before he could utter a single cry of alarm.

"Rex, it's me," Lucien whispered in a tone so low it was barely audible.

Rex froze in place, his mind moving at a glacial pace. He was on a hard floor, his valise under his head, and his boots still on his feet. He'd fallen asleep after taking the first watch during their roadside stop. The day before, Lord Audley had ordered Rex to drive Lucien to Amiens as fast as possible.

Lucien shifted enough to allow the shaft of wan light coming in through the broken shutter to illuminate the edge of his face. "Bad news, mate. We've got company."

Lucien's words woke Rex better than any alarm could have done. Rex blinked twice to clear his vision and Lucien removed his hand.

"I should have known something was wrong when the bridge was out," Lucien muttered under his breath. "Those timbers were still smoking."

Rex knew the one he meant. All that had been left of the temporary wooden structure were some blackened boulders and broken timber edges. Lucien had chalked it up to the map being out of date and the men had rerouted as best as they could, their alternative path taking them closer to the shifting borders between the two sides.

Mud patches, a flat tyre, and a fallen tree had all conspired to lengthen their journey until Lucien decided they had no choice but to camp overnight.

With practiced ease, Rex pulled into a crouch without making a sound. He followed Lucien to the window, making sure to keep low so they wouldn't be visible from the outside.

Outside, the first rays of dawn cast a pale glow over the surrounding landscape. Not that there was much to see other than overgrown fields of wheat mixed with wild grass. If the cloying heat in the air lasted longer than a few days, the field would soon be yellow.

There, near the small copse of trees, Rex spotted an extra shadow. A man-sized shadow.

Rex leaned close to Lucien and asked, "How many?"

Lucien raised three fingers.

"Friendly?"

"I've been watching them sneak closer for the last five minutes. No allied soldiers would work that hard to keep from being noticed, especially given that car of yours is easily recognisable as one of ours."

Rex couldn't fault his logic. Personal vehicles were almost non-existent at the front. Rex's Cadillac Type 57 had been a strategic gift from his father to keep him out of the trenches. It had worked, making Rex the official messenger overnight.

"What should we do? Wait them out?"

Lucien raised his pistol and aimed it out the window, squeezing off a warning shot at whomever was stalking them.

Satisfied, he dropped. "That should make them more cautious. We don't have much time and we can't stay here. We'll be sitting ducks in the daylight."

Rex glanced around the space and nodded his agreement. The abandoned farmhouse was little more than a long, narrow room with a door and a few windows. Neither man dared to touch the rotten shutters. The back shutters hung at an odd angle, providing a gap where they could see out. The little furniture left was broken.

No one knew where they were. As far as they were aware, there were no troops nearby. Any thoughts of sitting tight and waiting it out were for naught.

Rex took a deep breath and centred his thoughts until his mind was free from the terrifying grip of molten fear. He waited for Lucien to set forth a plan.

"I've assessed all our options. If we both run for the car, they'll hit one of us. We have to split up."

"One out the back and one out the front?"

"Of a sort," Lucien replied, "But it doesn't end there. Enemy presence here changes everything. I still have to get this message to Amiens, but it is equally urgent that you go back to Le Touquet. You have to tell Lord Audley we have a leak."

Rex goggled. He was in way over his head.

"Our destination was top secret. Only way someone could have found us is if they knew where to look. Just my luck. Of all the times to request a day's delay so I could get married. They had twenty-four-hour notice to put together a plan of their own."

Rex couldn't string his thoughts together enough to form a full sentence. Everything was happening too fast, and the cloying humidity wasn't helping. "Married? Yesterday?"

"Yes, to a nurse here... a family friend," he clarified. "My

he shoved the gear into neutral. He twisted around, pulling a knee onto the seat to give himself a better view.

Lucien lurched drunkenly and glanced down, staring at the hand hovering above his stomach. It was dark with blood. He coughed again and nearly choked.

Some part of Rex's brain recognised that the injury was fatal. A chest wound, so far from help. Even if they escaped their predicament, he'd never get Lucien back in time.

Another shot, this time aimed at him. It sliced through Rex's left arm, pain licking upward like a rush of flames.

Rex dropped in his seat, but never lifted his gaze from Lucien. If they were to die, they would not do so alone. Each would bear witness to the other's death.

Lucien chose a different ending. He stumbled sideways, swinging widely to face Rex, and waved for him to go. Then, despite his deadly injury, Lucien rushed ahead, drawing a rattle of enemy fire, and leaving the way clear for Rex to escape.

Rex pressed on the gas, fuelled as much by fear as by the sound of his name being shouted in a German accent.

He didn't let himself think about the man he'd left behind. His heroic deed. His final steps.

He drove faster than he had ever done before. His tyres slid on the mud. More than once, he nearly ran off the road. He could feel his heartbeat in his chest, head, and injured arm. It raced until it felt as though each beat began before the previous had finished.

It took a long while for him to realise that no one gave chase. His enemy had accomplished their task. They'd known exactly when and where to pick off the two men.

That was when the rain broke, showering upon Rex's head and shoulders. He was too exhausted to stop and struggle with the convertible top. By then, Rex was numb to all thought but getting back to Le Touquet. No one knew where he was. If he didn't make it back to camp, he, too, was dead. He bandaged his arm as best as he could and ignored the pain.

Against the grey sky, the faint outlines of the seaside village slowly grew more and more dense until he could see bricks and stone. As he approached the first edge of their defence, he shouted his name and rank, his voice sounding oddly high-pitched to his water-logged ears as he coasted to a stop. His car was recognisable enough for them to know he was a friend.

By the time someone came to his aid, he looked more like a spectre than a man. The rain, blood, and sweat had smeared into a thick paste caking his skin. He trembled, weak from blood loss and shock, as the guard shouted for a medic.

Waves of black crashed over him, threatening to steal him away from consciousness. As welcome as an escape might have been, with sheer grit Rex held it at bay.

He grabbed hold of the arm of the nurse washing his face, her blonde hair and emerald eyes swimming in and out of view. "Ambushed. Someone sold us out. Tell Audley," he begged, no longer needing to keep his failed mission a secret.

"Shh," she cooed. "Don't fight it, sir. It will be easier if you pass out."

Rex wanted to heed her words more than anything else in his life, especially when a doctor prodded the wound in his arm. He sucked in a breath, his universe shrinking until only his arm existed.

But he could not let go without delivering his last message. If he never woke again, someone else had to know the truth. He blinked until his vision cleared enough to see the nurse again. Light haloed around her head and blinded him from her features.

"Tell Lord Audley Lucien is dead. Message never made it to Amiens."

Chapter 3
The Viscountess Finds Her Voice

The constant drone of weary moans, half-choked sobs, and pleas for pain meds were so omnipresent that Dora hardly noticed them anymore. She couldn't say the same for the waxy touch of dead flesh or the horror of watching another young man die in front of her eyes.

The medical officer slid his hand over the boy's face, closing his eyes for the last time, and then nodded at Dora. "Pull the sheet over his head and then see to Sergeant Galliford. He's due for another check of his bandages."

The doctor turned his back, both literally and figuratively, on the body of the man he couldn't save.

Dora wished she could do the same. That carefully constructed wall she'd built around her heart had come tumbling down two weeks earlier when she'd heard the injured man pronounce Lucien dead. How she'd stayed at his side while the medic dug the bullet from his arm, she'd never know. The only explanation was that she'd somehow gone out of body, her mind drifting elsewhere while her steady hands offered bandages and clean water.

Inga's lips flattened, and she sucked in a breath of understanding. "Another demand for you to return home?"

"Got it in one. Going from wed to widowed in the span of a day is a tarnish I won't soon shed. Lucien wasn't the only one who died. He took my dreams of freedom with him."

Inga leaned over and patted her friend on the leg. "You're an adult, Dora. Your mother can hardly force you to comply with her wishes, no matter how well-intentioned they might be."

Dora's sharp bark of laughter burst out before she could stop it. "Oh Inga! Darling, darling Inga. You really have no idea, do you? When the Duchess of Dorset gets an idea in her head, no one short of the king himself can stop her. And I hardly think His Royal Highness is going to intervene on my behalf."

Inga shook her head. "Duchess or no, her power doesn't extend to the battlefield, Dora."

"No, but my father is one of the few men holding the purse-strings. A whispered word in the right ear and suddenly a shipment of ammunition, or worse, gets delayed. Rations are hard enough to come by."

"Is your father the sort of man who would punish an entire regiment in order to force his daughter's hand? Could your mother look at herself in the mirror, knowing the cost of her request?"

Dora levelled her gaze on Inga. "My father would issue threats, but stop short of enforcing them. As for my mother? To save her child? What would you do if you were a mother? What price would you deem too high to bring your child home to safety?"

Inga had no reply.

Dora lowered her head, finally noticing the deep red stains on her apron and the scent of copper in the air. She needed to change it, or at the very least, rinse it before the stains set in.

Inga's heavy sigh caught her attention.

"When will you go?"

"I should have already left. Two ships home have come and gone. I fear next time, Lord Audley will order me to leave."

"So, why haven't you gone?" Inga leaned forward and dropped her voice low. "Have you come up with another plan? Do you need help?"

Dora smiled and shook her head, still unable to believe her luck at making friends with such an exceptional woman. Inga was a nice middle-class woman, spinster daughter of a banker in Manchester. Despite her Germanic first name, she was as British as they came. Like Dora, she'd heeded the call to arms and had convinced her father to put her dowry toward the war effort. She'd raised enough funds from her community to pay for a cohort of women to join her in the hospital wards.

Although their worlds were now identical, and both came from a life of privilege, Inga had no way of grasping what it meant to be the hoyden daughter of a Duke. When war broke out, her parents declared her safest where she was, at school in the Swiss Alps. She'd had no funds, but she hadn't let that stop her.

Dora had resorted to sneaking away from her finishing school under the cover of darkness, after her friends had chipped in their pin money to pay her way. She'd written home to reassure her parents she was safe, but kept her actual location a secret until she'd arrived at the hospital in Le Touquet.

Lord Audley, Duke of Montagu, was one of the few men on this earth willing to stand up to her father. Dora had thanked her lucky stars when she'd learnt he was in charge. Most likely, he'd allowed her to stay because he knew it would tweak her father's nose. However, his goodwill wasn't without end.

Dora had nothing she could offer, and no leverage to hold over his head the way she'd done with Lucien.

Yet she resisted. Sure as the sun rises, she'd have little

trouble eventually landing on her feet. But she could not turn her back and walk away from this camp, leaving Lucien's murderer unpunished. That was exactly how she viewed the situation. It may have been a German soldier who pulled the trigger, but he'd never have found Lucien if someone hadn't told him exactly where to look.

Which brought her back to Inga's question. What was her plan? That she needed help was a given, but this was far removed from her childhood spying exploits.

"I have money," Inga admitted, taking care not to meet Dora's eyes. "You can escape into the countryside. Hide out until the war ends. Then go to America. You have family there, right? On your mother's side?"

It was a reasonable suggestion, no matter how much it galled Dora to consider taking money from someone so much less wealthy than her. It was one thing to take a collection from the daughters of Europe's richest families. It was another to leave Inga in a foreign country without a shilling to her name.

She'd joked with Lucien about her bank-robbing cousins and other nooses dangling from her family tree. Perhaps she could get the funds another way. Her brothers had made sure she was an excellent hand at cards.

If she made it to America, her grandmother would be delighted to take her in. A titled young lady, and a pretty one at that. She'd slip a silken cord around her neck and pull it tighter until Dora capitulated and married a railroad baron or bank scion, settling into a house in the Upper East Side.

Rage burned the back of Dora's throat, her gorge rising at the thought. Out of the fire, into the line of fire, and off to the firing squad. Her dreams buried six feet underground.

Just like Lucien.

Dora doubted Lucien's was the only life lost. Conversations about missing medical equipment and ruined bandages floated up from the depths of her memories. How much damage was this traitor causing?

She curled her hands around the edge of her stained apron, gripping the coarse material until it creaked and threatened to tear. Her voice was barely louder than a whisper, despite the steel lying underneath it.

"I will not go until I avenge Lucien. Keep your money and help me with this instead."

Inga met her eyes, looking deep as though she were taking her measure. "I will help you with anything, Dora, but I fear this is beyond us. Besides, it will come out in the end. These things always do."

Dora didn't back down. "That isn't good enough for me. It isn't good enough for them," she said, waving at the stone wall at their back. "The beds inside are full. You know as well as I that they are more often freed by death than by healing. And now, a traitor in our midst! Who will they doom next? It could be any of us."

"Yet you think outing a traitor to be a safe undertaking?"

Dora refused to listen. She reached over and took Inga's hands, closing them in her grasp. Her expression was free of all pretence, while her eyes sparkled with defiance and determination.

"We pledged to do our utmost to save these men. I must do this and do it fast. And I cannot do it alone."

Inga tightened her jaw. "You put your life at risk, and mine. What makes you think you can identify this person before they catch on to what you're doing?"

"Two reasons. First, we're two women, nurses not soldiers, about as far removed from the rank and file as you can get here. Who will suspect us of even trying?"

Inga narrowed her eyes, still unconvinced. "And the second?"

he'd been ill, but near death? He was suddenly grateful his memories of that first week after being shot were lost.

He raised his head and met the medical officer's gaze. "And now?"

The doctor shrugged. "The fear is the same, but it won't be this injury that kills you."

Rex couldn't help but laugh at the honest response. It was true. Given their proximity to the enemy, none of them was guaranteed a long lifespan. Despite that, Rex was champing at the bit to take up his charge again. While he didn't relish dodging bullets or spending days in the wet, muddy trenches, he was not about to abandon his duty.

"How long until I can return to active duty?" Rex asked, fumbling with the button on his shirt. It was proving to be surprisingly difficult to do up with only one hand. His wince of pain didn't go unnoticed by the keen eyes of the medical officer.

"If I were up to me, you'd keep that arm clean, dry, and still for at least another week, perhaps two. However, your return date is up to Lord Audley. I've orders to send you to his office. Immediately," he added.

Rex took this news in stride, mostly because he knew it would be easier to convince his superior of his health than the doctor. Lord Audley could hardly be described as brash, but he was realistic enough to know that a mostly healed commander was as good as it got after four years of war.

His attempt to walk away hit upon a snag. His right foot was strangely heavier than the left. A glance downward explained why. Hanging from his shoestrings was a marmalade-coloured kitten.

The doctor hardly batted an eyelash at the sight of an invader in his hospital. "New recruit, Captain?"

Rex frowned at the kitten, not the least because it was tangled in his laces. He leaned over, biting back a grimace when the movement jarred his injured arm, and then scooped the kitten with his good hand. "Bit young, but determined, as you can see. I'll return him to the stables on my way to see Lord Audley."

"See that you do," the officer replied, before turning his back to proceed to his next patient.

Rex somehow kept a straight face as he exited the room at a clip, ignoring the nurse who giggled at the sight of a soldier cuddling a kitten.

His severe expression offered no hint of his familiarity with the tiny animal, which had befriended him a few days earlier. It had been late in the night, and some poor sod's muffled sobs woke Rex from his sleep. He'd shifted his leg under the covers, accidentally dislodging the little creature curled next to his feet. It had taken little encouragement for the kitten to crawl up his torso and under the covers. They'd both enjoyed the company.

But now playtime was over, and the kitten needed to go back to where it belonged. The stables loomed ahead, a flurry of men and horses marking their location. Rex strode closer, having to watch his step for more reasons than one. It took a moment for his eyes to adjust to the dark interior of the makeshift building.

Inside, it was an organised chaos. Oversized wagon wheels, giant horses, and men dashing left and right filled the space. Rex surveyed the stables and then glanced down at the kitten.

The cat threaded its claws through the fabric of his shirt, stopping short of drawing blood. "Mew?" it asked.

Rex didn't have to be an animal whisperer to know what the cat was asking. He spun around and exited the same way he'd come in. "You're lucky I'm billeted in a room and not camping in a tent."

The kitten purred in response.

After a quick detour to his quarters to drop off his new

roommate, Rex turned his mind to his upcoming meeting. If anything, he was surprised it had taken Lord Audley this long to demand an audience. Had he not got the message that Lucien's death was no accident? Or had Lord Audley chalked his ravings up to the madness of fever and exhaustion?

Rex wished for a moment that he knew, before resigning himself to dealing with whatever outcome he found. He may not remember much of anything from his first days in the sick ward, but his recollection of the events surrounding Lucien's death was clear as day. They'd been funnelled away from help, plain and simple. Someone knew when and where they were headed, and had intervened to keep Lord Audley's secret communiqué from reaching its destination.

The command office of Lord Audley sat on the top floor of the former Hotel de Ville. Reaching it required passing through a gauntlet of lower ranked officers. Rex knew the other officers and sergeants well enough that no one asked him why he was there. They did, however, inquire into his health and mention how glad they were to see him back on his feet.

By the time Rex reached the desk of Audley's soldier-servant, his forehead was dripping with sweat. He surreptitiously wiped it clean before clearing his throat to get the man's attention.

"Captain Bankes-Fernsby reporting in as requested," he announced.

The sergeant made a point of checking his list before rising to his feet. He crossed to the next door and gave a quick rap. After a muffled reply from inside, he opened the door and announced Rex's name.

"He will see you now, Captain."

This was far from the first time he'd been inside this office. As one of the senior officers, he'd spent many an evening sitting at the large meeting table in the middle of the room, poring over maps. Even now, the table's surface was completely obscured by papers showing troop movements and supply lines.

Rex wanted to stop and check what had happened since his injury, but he forced his eyes to remain focused on the lean man seated behind the scarred wooden desk.

"Lord Audley, you asked to see me, sir?"

"Take a seat, Rex." Lord Audley lifted his gaze from his latest missive and settled it on his injured captain. Audley's thick grey hair and moustache spoke as much to his seniority as the bars on the front of his shirt. His sharp blue eyes revealed keen intelligence. His mouth was set in a firm line, neither happy nor sad. "How goes the recovery?"

"Fine, sir," Rex assured him. "It was hardly more than a scratch."

Lord Audley acknowledged his highly inaccurate statement with a deadpan look. "The medical officer described it somewhat differently, and suggested I assign you desk duty for two more weeks."

Desk duty? Rex couldn't stop the sneer of distaste from crossing his face. "You know how the doctors are, sir. I'm fine."

"Your attempts to hold your left arm perfectly still suggest otherwise. I'm not sending you off gallivanting in that car of yours until you can move without wincing." Lord Audley motioned to the door behind Rex. "Sergeant Grimsby will provide you with the paperwork for your next assignment. There's a large shipment due in, and I need someone to oversee the setup of a new storage facility."

Rex knew better than to argue. Still, the assignment grated on him. Was it truly due to his injury, or a reflection of a more sinister sentiment?

Lord Audley had already returned to his own paperwork, having considered the matter closed. It was only when Rex failed to follow his instruction that he looked up again.

our command post. Ignore me at your peril. At everyone's peril. Who knows who will die next?"

Rex's impassioned speech achieved his objective. Lord Audley rested his elbows on his desk and stared into his crossed hands, deep in thought. No longer was he issuing denials.

At that moment, Rex saw another way in which he could aid his fellow soldiers. "Allow me to ferret out the identity of our traitor. I am injured. No one will question if you leave me on the sidelines for an extra week or two."

"You believe you could accomplish this, Captain? You, who has never conducted an investigation?"

"My experience of sitting at death's doorstep will make me a fast learner, sir." Rex sensed Lord Audley was weakening, so he pressed his point. "You said the men who knew the details of the mission were your most trusted. Whom can you ask to investigate them? You know my own motives. Please, don't put anyone else in jeopardy. Let me find the truth, whatever it may be."

Lord Audley lowered his hands until they came to rest of the top of his desk. He looked Rex full in the face. "Very well. You have my permission. I will tell the sergeant to cancel the orders for your assignment. In the meantime, you report to me, and me only. Is that clear?"

"Clear as the crystal goblets on my mother's dinner table, sir."

"Good. Here are the names of the other two men. One is the sergeant sitting outside my door. The other is Major Edgewell, my second in command."

Chapter 5
A Picnic With A Purpose

Dora sashayed into her shared accommodation to see what was taking her roommate so long. Instead of putting her shoes on or combing her hair, Inga lay sprawled across her bed with her arm covering her eyes.

"Why aren't you getting ready to go?" Dora demanded.

"Go where?" Inga replied, her voice muffled with sleep. "The red lamp district and estaminet are off limits to us. The only entertainment venue in town is currently in use as a hospital. After six days of work, we've got a mere half-day to ourselves. Let me rest."

Dora crossed her arms and surveyed her friend. Between her pallor and the fact that she was lying on top of her covers, still fully dressed in her nursing uniform, there was no question of Inga's exhaustion. That didn't mean Dora could afford to take pity on her. Not if she wanted to solve Lucien's murder before her family dragged her home.

She crossed to her friend's side and peeled her hand away from her face. Inga opened one eye wide enough to glare at Dora.

"You can sleep when you're dead... or after I'm gone. But

not today. We've got more important things to do than lie around and let the world pass us by. Get dressed before we're late."

After a moment of weighing her options, Inga sighed heavily and forced herself to sit up. "Where are we going, and more importantly, will there be any alcohol there?"

Dora ignored the second question, focusing on the first while pulling appropriate clothing from Inga's chest of drawers. "Put this on. We're going on a picnic."

"A picnic? In the middle of a bloody war? And I do mean that literally."

Dora glared at her friend. "Given how warm it is, Theresa Edgewell decided to move the afternoon games to the boardwalk. She thought it would be good for all of us, patients and nurses alike, to enjoy what little cool air there is coming across the Channel."

Inga took the proffered summer dress, but continued to grouse under her breath while she changed her clothes. Dora busied herself with brushing her hair and pinching her cheeks. It wasn't so much that she wanted anyone to find her attractive, as she was determined to avoid being described as deathly pale.

"I'm as good as I'm going to get," Inga pronounced. "I'm also now awake enough to question your motives. You normally avoid these types of social events, so I assume you have a specific purpose for dragging me out of my bed. Beyond basking in the sunshine," she added.

"Nothing gets by your clever mind, does it? We do indeed have a deeper reason for attending. I heard that Lord Audley will be stopping by to say hello to the group."

Inga arched an eyebrow. "Lord Audley? That is high company. Although, I daresay for someone of your social status, rubbing elbows with a duke is hardly a notable occasion. So again, why are we going?"

"Because he is my prime suspect."

Dora's words lingered in the air. Inga goggled, sure she had misheard, until Dora took pity on her and explained her rationale.

"Lucien was originally due to have two days of leave following our wedding. However, Lord Audley called him to his office only a few hours before the ceremony. There, he passed along the assignment. He wanted him to go straight away. It took all of Lucien's charm to talk him into letting him wait a day."

"I admit that I am not *au fait* with the chain of command, but surely receiving orders directly from the camp commander is out of the ordinary."

"That was what I said when Lucien told me," Dora agreed. "It was a top secret mission, Inga. Lucien didn't want to tell me anything. If I hadn't held his feet to the proverbial fire by threatening to go to Lord Audley myself and demand the day of leave, Lucien never would have told me what little he did. He was clear. It was a two-man mission, therefore he couldn't back out without endangering the entire plan."

Inga opened her mouth to ask another question, but Dora waved her off before she could get the words out.

"I'll tell you everything later. But first, we've got a social to attend."

The women pasted droll smiles across their faces and left their room for the newly designated picnic spot.

Major Edgewell's wife had wielded her considerable influence to convince the junior officers to set up some tents near the seaside. Brighton Pavilion, it was not, but Dora couldn't fault Theresa for her attempt to add some gaiety to the scene.

Two sisters from York sang along while an injured soldier strummed his guitar. Another cluster of individuals laughed at their attempts to throw horseshoes. Dora half-wished she could

she was facilitating their transfer among the recovering men had been priceless.

That thought cast a pall over Dora's day. She excused herself from the small group, saying she'd fetch a fresh pitcher of water.

Thus freed from the encumbrance of conversation, Dora let her gaze skim the faces of the surrounding people, searching for any sign of Lord Audley's grey hair amongst the younger army men. She was so intent on looking around that she failed to notice when a man stepped into her path.

"Oof," she huffed, with a distinct lack of elegance, as she stumbled sideways. A firm hand grasped her arm to keep her from falling. She looked up and saw a pair of brilliant sapphire eyes staring back at her.

"Terribly sorry, miss..." Rex blurted, waiting for the unfamiliar beauty to fill in her name.

"My fault," Dora squeaked. She lowered her eyes to the ground, mumbled an apology, and made quick work of her escape. She bustled into the nearest tent and failed to notice the way Rex's eyes followed her path.

The last time she'd seen those eyes, they'd been bright with fever, seeming almost to glow against the layer of mud on his cheeks.

Lord Reginald Bankes-Fernsby, or Captain Rex, as the men called him. She had another name for him.

Lone survivor.

He'd come home and her Lucien had not. She tried desperately not to begrudge the man his continued existence, but it was proving easier said than done. She'd heard the stories of his desperate getaway. Knowing Lucien had ordered Rex to leave him behind hadn't helped.

As much as Dora wanted to keep half an eye on him, now

wasn't the time. Fortunately, the arrival of Lord Audley provided a distraction from that line of thinking.

Usually, when the camp's senior commander was around, Dora made herself scarce. Not because she was doing anything wrong, but mostly to keep him from remembering she was there. There was no hope of remaining incognito around someone who had known her father since his days at Oxford.

She took full advantage of the shadows inside the water tent to spy on her prey without making him aware he was under surveillance.

Lord Audley's arrival had a sobering effect on the spirit of the attendees. Conversations trailed off, groups dispersed, and backs straightened as every soldier within sight showed their respect.

All that was to be expected when Lord Audley entered a room. He wasn't just their leader. He was a peer of the realm, Knight of the Garter, and trusted advisor to the King. His station so far exceeded the vast majority of his troops that meeting him was akin to seeing a member of the royal family pass before them.

How someone of such great importance ended up overseeing logistics in a French port, far from the major battlefields, was the question sitting on top of Dora's list. Although her father regularly unleashed blistering complaints about how vexing Lord Audley was to him personally, Dora hadn't heard any rumours questioning his dedication to crown and country.

And yet, here he was.

Based on the knowledge she'd gained while eavesdropping from behind the shelves in her father's study, Dora knew there were only three reasons why a duke ended up in exile. She excluded the most obvious answer without hesitation. There was no way Lord Audley had engaged in activities embarrassing to the crown, unless he had bored a host of people to death.

The second option was that there were questions about Lord Audley's loyalties, but not enough evidence to warrant barring him from the war front outright. Men such as that tended to be found out rather quickly, especially by those close around them. Therefore, Dora ignored the reactions of the general troops and instead focused on the officers.

Given the informal setting, there were few to hand. Dora noted their positions and watched carefully as they took turns paying their regards. Some smiled. Others kept stoic expressions. All, however, showed nothing but genuine respect —from their attention to his words, the way their gazes followed him around the impromptu social event, to their jostling for turns to say hello.

What advantage would Lord Audley gain from sending Lucien to his death? Assuming the damaged supplies were related, it made even less sense Audley would be involved.

Dora sensed someone coming up behind her, the light scent of her soap identifying her as well as her voice.

"Notice anything so far?" Inga whispered.

Dora held still for a beat before giving a single nod of her head. "Two things, actually. Regardless of what it says on his paper orders, Lord Audley has another purpose for being stationed here, but I don't think he's our traitor."

Inga gave her friend a sideways glance, waiting for further explanation. When none came, she asked, "And the second?"

Dora inclined her head, motioning toward a young man standing off on his own, observing the crowd not unlike her. "Lord Rex is also up to something... but I'm not convinced his motives are as pure. He's the one I need to keep under watch."

Chapter 6
Uniformed and Undercover

Identifying a suspect was one thing. Investigating him was much more difficult, especially for a nurse positioned at the front. Dora's time was far from her own. Her family name and station carried no weight with the matrons overseeing the women's activities.

Dora and Inga reported in for their turn at duty, bright and early the next day. Dora's plan was relatively simple. At some point, she'd fake a swoon, claim heatstroke, and get permission to go lie down. As long as she returned to the hospital within a few hours, no one would come check on her. That was more than enough time to search Rex's quarters and find out his current assignment.

The effort she'd put into planning was all for naught. Who should walk into her hospital that morning but Rex himself. She was so startled by his sudden arrival that she nearly dropped the small basin of water she was carrying. Thankfully, she caught herself in time to prevent a double disaster of spilling dirty water and attracting Rex's attention.

After having literally run into him the day before, Dora was determined to avoid his gaze. If he was up to something, he'd be

platoon. The sergeant for that particular platoon was well known around camp thanks to his high-profile secondment. Shortly after Lord Audley arrived, one Sergeant Grimsby had gone from the front lines to the front desk.

As Lord Audley's servant-soldier, Sergeant Grimsby spent his every waking hour catering to the lord's whims. From pressing his uniform, to running missives, to ensuring his lordship's day remained on time, the sergeant had little time to himself.

Some might have questioned such dedication. Dora knew it wasn't altruism. Lord Audley's valet in England was heavily wrinkled and half blind. If Sergeant Grimsby played his cards right, he had a good chance of landing a permanent role in Lord Audley's household whenever the war ended.

If that weren't lure enough, Sergeant Grimsby had a better-than-average hope of surviving the war, given his permanent station some distance from the front lines.

But perhaps the sergeant had his eye on a faster payout, one with decidedly less work required. Dora knew that the man had a front row seat to all the camp communications. If Rex was looking for someone to tempt into betrayal, he couldn't do much better than Grimsby.

By the time Rex left for the day, Dora was more determined than ever to keep an eye on him. It was close enough to the end of her shift that she didn't have to rely on an excuse to leave. She caught Inga's eye again and gave a long, slow blink. Then, she gathered a handful of items to take to the washroom and departed without another word. Inga would cover should anyone question her early departure.

After dropping off the dirty linens, Dora spotted Rex's head and shoulders walking ahead of her, in the direction of the main command building. For a moment, she worried he'd go inside, making it difficult for her to follow unnoticed. Not impossible, mind you, but certainly a challenge which would require time to solve.

Her luck held when he lingered outside of the door, chatting with the guard on duty. Dora stepped into the shadows of the nearest building across the cobblestone street. A stack of crates provided her with a narrow hiding place. She ducked behind them, untied her apron, and rolled it into a tight ball. Satisfied she'd done as much as she could to mute her appearance and keep cool, she set up her watch.

Her expert eyes traced the lines of the main building. After months spent in hastily erected tents and churned up ground, she'd given a sigh of relief when she'd arrived in the small French village. The townspeople had been all too happy to hand over their buildings and stores to the allies in exchange for a promise of payment. Better them than the alternative. The enemy would spare them no coin. Some had remained to lend a hand while others had retreated further from the battle lines.

The command post was in what was once the town hall, or Hotel de Ville as the locals called it. The cheery rose paint was now stained and cracked, but the old dame wasn't completely ready to give up the ghost of her past purpose. There was a certain elegance to the rows of windows with their wooden shutters and gabled roof. The hands of the old clock set into the main gable inched their progress around the painted white face.

Dora's legs ached, as much from the long hours on her feet as from her hunched position. But still Rex stood out front, making conversation with one passerby after another. He was well-liked, none begrudging him a moment of their time. Watching him, one would think they were standing in the lobby of Claridge's instead of a French seaside village near the frontlines of war.

Dora shifted, willing the blood back into her tingling feet.

Her mind was fully occupied with the puzzle that was Lord Rex.

Her grumbling stomach and screaming calves gave a silent prayer of thanks when Rex finally abandoned his unofficial post of greeter. She was glad enough to get moving as she'd grown stiff enough that she had to force her feet to hurry to keep up. She kept her gaze fixed on her feet, lifting it only occasionally to track Rex's progress.

The man he walked beside was none other than Sergeant Grimsby himself.

Dora vowed to follow the pair wherever they went, whatever it took. Still, their destination tested her mettle.

The men took a sharp right and walked through the door of the church hall. What had once served spiritual sustenance to the masses now offered more earthly meals to the officers.

Dora waited a beat to make sure they didn't come back out again, and then spun around and ran as fast as she dared.

She flung open the door to her shared accommodation, startling Inga, and aimed straight for the small wardrobe. Inga looked on as Dora shoved aside her few plain navy dresses and reached instead for the drab green coat and trousers.

"You're really going to attempt this?" Inga asked, unable to keep the incredulity from her voice.

"Why else would I have wasted our candlelight hemming the trousers and taking in the waist?" Dora spun around, pointing at her back. "Are you going to sit there with your mouth hanging open or give me a hand?"

Inga knew better than to argue. She undid the buttons on her friend's dress and scooped the offending article from the floor when Dora let it slide off. While Dora donned Lucien's old uniform, now tailored to fit her to a tee, Inga cast her eye around their simple room. Men's clothing wouldn't be enough. Dora's baby-soft cheeks would never pass muster.

Dora, however, had a ready solution to that problem. With a practiced hand, she knotted her hair up and wiggled the cap into place, somehow making it look as though her hair was no longer than the nape of her neck. Make up darkened her wan skin tone into something sun-touched. She dragged her fingers through their small fireplace, gathering a dusting of ash, and shaded her chin and upper lip.

"You'll do," Inga pronounced.

"I'll have to, although heaven help me if I sweat. I've used too much time already."

Dora unlatched the window, slung both legs over the edge, and dropped from view. Inga finally understood why Dora had demanded they stay on the ground floor.

Dora slipped through the now dark streets like the ghost that she was in the dead man's clothes. When she laid eyes on the officer's mess hall, she slowed, lengthening her steps as she moderated her gait. She'd watched her brothers enough to know how a man's step differed from a woman's.

The spacious church hall was filled with line after line of wooden tables and chairs. At the top of the hour, it would fill to the seams with hungry, tired officers. Now, the room was mostly empty.

Inside, she grunted a hoarse greeting and picked up the offered plate of food. Dora forced her shoulders to hunch, portraying a man who was too tired for conversation. She needn't have worried. Everyone was exhausted by now, from the most senior officer in the room to the lowest lad wiping the tables. Few had the energy to keep up any kind of mindless chatter. That was, in part, what made Rex's efforts that day stand out.

Rex and Grimsby had chosen to sit on the far side. Dora shuffled over, keeping her back to the men as she sat down at the

Chapter 7
A Debate with a Duke

Dora didn't bother to change out of her borrowed clothing. This wasn't to be a social call, not that she thought she'd gain entry if it was. She wanted Lord Audley to see her as an equal, and not as some teary-eyed widow to pat on the back before hurrying on her way.

She knew exactly where he lived. Most of the officers were billeted in the smaller seaside hotels. Lord Audley resided in a nondescript, mid-sized row house near the centre of Le Touquet. Dora stealthily approached the narrow alley behind it. She stopped before unlatching the back gate and tugged on the neck of her shirt.

Was she really going to do this — break into the home of a duke, wearing a dead man's clothes? Until that moment, she had restricted her games of playacting and dressing up to family and friends. This was no childhood game, and Lord Audley wasn't a friend.

He wasn't exactly an enemy, either. They were on the same side. Surely he'd see her for what she was — a woman hellbent on seeking justice. She slipped into the shadows, her borrowed uniform making her invisible.

All the windows were dark, just as she expected. Every Tuesday evening, he paid a visit to his mistress. He always returned a little before midnight, long after his housekeeper turned in.

Dora slipped off her borrowed boots and tiptoed up the flagstone path. She had planned to pick the lock to the study door, but it was unlocked. That made sense. Who would dare to burgle the base commander's home?

She adjusted the glow of the gas lamp, casting one side of the room in deep shadows. When she was satisfied with the scene, she made herself comfortable for the wait. Adrenaline kept her from nodding off, but to be safe, she pulled one of Lucien's cigars from the metal holder in her breast pocket and twirled it between her fingers.

Thus it was that Dora was sitting in Lord Audley's favourite armchair when he returned to his lodging. A lit cigar trailed smoke into the air from where it hung between her fingertips. The smell was as distinct as the man who used to smoke them.

If Lord Audley was surprised to find a woman dressed as a man, sitting with her feet up in his study, he didn't let on. He poured himself a sniffer of brandy and claimed the seat opposite her, searching the shadows around her face with a wrinkled brow. Dora removed her cap, allowing her blonde locks to tumble free, and shifted until the light illuminated her features. His expression cleared as recognition hit.

"Viscountess, I see you've made yourself at home. To what do I owe the honour of your presence?"

Dora puffed the cigar, perfuming the air until the scent of Lucien filled the room like a ghost. Her mind whirled as she reexamined everything she knew of the man sitting across from her. He'd accepted a stranger in his home without a single cry of alarm. No man was that unflappable. She couldn't put her finger on what made him different.

Therefore, she blustered on. "I've come to ask your intentions, Lord Audley."

Lord Audley reclined against the back of his leather armchair and sipped his drink. "My immediate intentions are to get a few hours of sleep before I rise tomorrow morning and do it all again. But I assume you have something else in mind with your questions. Are you asking about my intentions regarding you?"

Dora tapped the ash from her cigar and gave him a bland look. Obviously, she wasn't here to inquire about his health.

"You are not the only one receiving missives from your family. Your dear father, the Duke of Dorset, has demanded your dismissal and return to England. If he hadn't suggested I was ignorant of your presence here, I might have complied. As it is, your role as a nurse had not slipped my notice. So, you might say that I'm weighing my options."

Dora processed his wooly reply, reading between the lines. "You've yet to determine what will tweak my father's nose more — allowing me to remain or assisting me with my escape."

"Indeed," he answered, raising his glass to toast in her direction. "Based on your current wardrobe choice, I presume you're leaning toward the latter?"

"Perhaps," she said, refusing to commit. "Before I go anywhere, there is the matter of my husband's death to resolve."

Lord Audley softened not one centimetre. He did, however, bristle when Dora blew a perfect smoke ring into the air. "Men die on these shores every day. I shouldn't need to remind you of that."

"None have died from cold-blooded murder, my lord. Lucien's death was no accident of war, nor a case of being in the wrong place at the wrong time. Someone leaked his departure plans to the enemy, all but ensuring his death."

Dora and Lord Audley stared at one another. Despite the

smoothed the stays over her flat stomach and spun around, turning her back on her friend. "Tighten me up, will you?"

Inga did as she asked, while grumbling, "It still seems ridiculous to me that you're having to dress for a social event when we're surrounded by military tents and army officers."

"It may look like a party from the outside, but Lord Audley's salons are more of a hotbed of information and opinions than anything else."

Inga's head snapped up. "He's held these before?"

"One every three to four months, give or take. He announces the dates with little notice to keep the huns from turning them into target practice for their aeroplanes. Lucien went a time or two and told me about them, so I know what to expect."

"And that is..."

"Lord Audley proposes a question for debate and watches carefully to see where the opinions of his guests land. Only his lordship knows what else he gathers from the events. For example, tonight he expects Rex to subtly question Major Edgewell. I'll watch the two of them, and everyone else. With any luck, someone will slip up and give us a hint of where we can find our traitor."

"Rex knows about you?"

Dora shook her head. "Oh no, absolutely not. And I intend to keep my distance from him. I doubt he'd welcome my involvement."

"I imagine not." Inga sat back and watched as Dora finished buttoning her shirt. "At least let me do something with your hair."

Dora let Inga mother her for as long as she could stand it, and then said her goodbyes. For once, she left through the front door rather than her bedroom window, and climbed into the motor car waiting out front. The soldier assigned to drive her to

Therefore, she blustered on. "I've come to ask your intentions, Lord Audley."

Lord Audley reclined against the back of his leather armchair and sipped his drink. "My immediate intentions are to get a few hours of sleep before I rise tomorrow morning and do it all again. But I assume you have something else in mind with your questions. Are you asking about my intentions regarding you?"

Dora tapped the ash from her cigar and gave him a bland look. Obviously, she wasn't here to inquire about his health.

"You are not the only one receiving missives from your family. Your dear father, the Duke of Dorset, has demanded your dismissal and return to England. If he hadn't suggested I was ignorant of your presence here, I might have complied. As it is, your role as a nurse had not slipped my notice. So, you might say that I'm weighing my options."

Dora processed his wooly reply, reading between the lines. "You've yet to determine what will tweak my father's nose more — allowing me to remain or assisting me with my escape."

"Indeed," he answered, raising his glass to toast in her direction. "Based on your current wardrobe choice, I presume you're leaning toward the latter?"

"Perhaps," she said, refusing to commit. "Before I go anywhere, there is the matter of my husband's death to resolve."

Lord Audley softened not one centimetre. He did, however, bristle when Dora blew a perfect smoke ring into the air. "Men die on these shores every day. I shouldn't need to remind you of that."

"None have died from cold-blooded murder, my lord. Lucien's death was no accident of war, nor a case of being in the wrong place at the wrong time. Someone leaked his departure plans to the enemy, all but ensuring his death."

Dora and Lord Audley stared at one another. Despite the

differences in age and sex, Dora had the strangest sensation that she was looking at someone just like her. She tilted her chin up and refused to budge.

Lord Audley tossed back his head and barked a laugh. "Murder? Does such a crime exist in these circumstances? Come now, Viscountess. You are overwrought."

Dora sat up straight and crushed her cigar into the ashtray. "Overwrought? Do you see any signs of hysteria in my countenance? I am nothing of the sort. You have a traitor in your inner circle. Do you intend to do something about it, or are you too blinded by your own preeminence to admit such a thing might happen?"

She prepared herself to feel the burn of his fury. Instead, his voice became icy. "Are we removing our gloves? So be it. I've heard enough tales of you over the years, claiming you possess a modicum of intelligence and the spirit of a wild horse. And yet, during your time in my camp, you've kept your head down and worked as hard as anyone else. I'd nearly decided those tales were gross exaggerations... but then Viscount Lucien came to me to tell me of your plans to marry."

Dora arched one perfectly formed eyebrow, unable to guess where he was going with that remark.

"Spare me any proclamations of love and undying affection. Tracking rumours is my trade. Lucien was the subject of plenty. But," he said, "I have no interest in unmasking your grand plan. I'm sure Lucien dying within a day wasn't part of it. Therefore, you are angry, and wish to blame someone. If you want that someone to be me, fine. But my patience ends there."

Dora was unmoved. "Nowhere in that monologue was a denial of my assertion. I'm right, aren't I? You are looking for a leak. I have a suggestion."

"A suggestion? You toss this out as though we are playing a dinner party game and not discussing a hanging offence." Lord

Audley chuckled. "By all means, Viscountess. I can't wait to hear what you've discovered in between emptying bedpans and mopping fevered brows."

The answer was on the tip of her tongue, but Dora reined herself in. She could blurt her reply and offer her logic. Lord Audley would pat her on her head and send her on her way. She'd be on the next ship home before she could even say her goodbyes.

Lord Audley only had time for people who could provide him with something he valued. That wasn't money or fame. He valued intelligence. And if Dora was nothing else, she was terribly, terribly clever.

Instead of giving the expected reply, she chose to interpret Lord Audley's invitation to share her thoughts in the widest possible way.

"I know the outcome of the war will be decided in the next six months."

Lord Audley rolled his eyes. "People have been saying that since the first shot was fired."

Dora marched onward with her explanation, ignoring his interruption. "The Soviet armistice last year did our side no favours. The Germans made a valiant effort to crush our spirits with their spring offensive. Thousands of good men died under their barrage of bullets, my brother included. But I can't help but notice that their victories have slowed. Their efforts, like bombing our hospitals, reek of desperation. I think I know why."

"Enlighten me," Lord Audley invited. The quirk of his lips revealed his enjoyment.

"There are many examples throughout history, from as far east as the battle of Shangdang in 260BC, to Hannibal against the Romans, and as recent as our once-feared enemy Napoleon. Wars are won and lost based on the supply lines. Having spent time near the front, I know how impossible it is to move men and goods overnight. General Ludendorff made the classic mistake of prioritising speed above all else. I suspect his gambit is failing because his men are hungry and his supplies are short."

Lord Audley steepled his fingers. "Why do you think the Germans would do such a thing?"

"Because the Yanks are coming with reinforcements. Anyone here can't help but notice how our ranks are swelling. As far as gambits go, I can't fault Ludendorff's attempt to force a quick end. He clearly underestimated our ability to defend key ground. He underestimated men like you, Lord Audley."

Lord Audley shook his head. "My importance is greatly overstated."

"In between emptying bed pans and smoothing covers, as you say, I noted how often battalions were reassigned to the front. Despite the desperate need for more men, you've retained a handful of our best here. Those men leave in small groups, disappearing for days at a time. They aren't going to the trenches."

The tick in his clenched jaw betrayed his interest. "How do you figure that?"

"They're hardly immune to injury, but not a single one has been exposed to gas or returned with wounds typical of battle. This is why I breathed a sigh of relief when you took Lucien under your wing. Much good that it did him in the end," she muttered. "But to return to the present. Time is of the essence. I suspect your men are relaying orders to the front, or information too secret to be entrusted to the normal communication channels. You sent Lucien on a mission on the day after our wedding. You mean to end this war before the winter snows set in. I intend to stay here until the end. Is that enough to convince you of the value of my insights or need I say more before you will listen?"

Lord Audley's gaze had sharpened as she spoke and colour crept up his cheeks. "Lucien told you..."

"He told me nothing, Lord Audley, except that his last mission was a direct assignment from you, and any thoughts I had of lobbying for a delay were pointless. I have a sharp eye, an excellent—if somewhat unorthodox—education, and the ability to hold my tongue. You have nothing to fear from me. Let me help. For Lucien's sake," she added.

Lord Audley held stock still as he considered all she'd said.

Dora hardly dared to breathe. The longer she sat, the more momentous the occasion became. Lord Audley's expression revealed nothing of his reaction. She felt herself teetering on the brink of something, but it could go either way. Maybe he'd listen... maybe he'd consign her to the next transport home.

It took all her self-control to keep from trembling.

"You say you have a suspect," he said, finally.

Dora nodded and opened her mouth to answer, but he waved her off.

"No, don't tell me yet. Before you list a name, I want you to walk me through everything you've done to gather this information. Prove to me this is more than an idle guess."

That is exactly what Dora did. For what might have been the first time in her life, she was completely forthcoming. There was no advantage to holding back. She needed every card up her sleeve to convince Lord Audley to give her suspicion the full weight of his attention.

She finished her tale with her late night arrival in his own home, at the end giving him the name of her top suspect.

"I'm beginning to think I was even more wrong than I thought. The rumours of your intelligence have drastically underestimated your abilities, to say nothing of your chameleon ways. Parading around as a decorated officer, during wartime, at a command post? Even the enemy wouldn't dare. And yet, you've pulled it off."

"So you will investigate Lord Rex?" Dora asked.

"No," he answered, again holding up a hand to forestall her. "Not that I'm dismissing your suspicion. You were missing a key fact, which I will now share. Lord Rex came to me, not two days ago, with the same request. I assigned him the task of looking into my inner circle to see if there are any weaknesses. The fact that you cottoned on to his activities so quickly speaks as much to your abilities as to him being out of his depth."

"Then call him off," Dora countered. "He has all the subtlety of Big Bertha on the battlefield. He's more likely to scare off a traitor than unmask them."

"I could stand him down, but there is another alternative. If you are agreeable to continuing with your own investigation, that is."

Dora tilted her head to the side. "I'm listening."

"Follow along behind him. See what he misses and tread the paths he overlooks. Consider it a test."

"A test for what?" Dora asked before she could bite her tongue.

"Pass it and you will see. Return to your lodging and get some rest. I'll send a missive tomorrow with more information."

Dora leapt to her feet and executed a flawless salute, despite her sock-feet and borrowed clothes. It wasn't until she was halfway back to her room that the potential downsides of her actions crossed her mind.

Spying on her family members, dressing up, and quoting facts from the history books were one thing. Conducting an actual undercover investigation was quite another.

She'd spent hours in the library, reading stories of women who dared to stray beyond the stiff confines of society. Some rose to the challenge, leaving legacies that outlived them by centuries. How many other women had stood in those same shoes and balked rather than take the risk?

A line from Chaucer's Canterbury Tales floated to the forefront of her mind.

"I will arise and take a chance, too, by my faith! Nothing ventured, nothing gained, or so men say."

Chapter 8
A Salon of Snakes

Dora surveyed her reflection. She'd always been slender, but the long hours and meagre rations had leeched away what little padding she'd had before the war. However, all the hard work in the hospital wards had brought one benefit. Her arms and legs had grown strong.

Not that anyone back home would see that as a good thing.

Young women weren't meant to be muscled. Lifting her embroidery and tinkling the piano keys were the only acceptable form of exercise. But maybe that would change, once this damnable war ended and they could all go home.

Dora intended to spearhead the charge for greater freedom and new opportunities. But first, the matter at hand. She had a murder to investigate and a traitor to unmask. That was the only reason she had accepted Lord Audley's invitation.

"You truly are a glutton for punishment," Inga said, wrinkling her nose at the corset in Dora's hands.

"Don't remind me. It's my least favourite of the seven deadly sins as it is. Goodness knows how hard Lucien would laugh to see me trussed into a corset for a formal party." Dora smoothed the stays over her flat stomach and spun around, turning her back on her friend. "Tighten me up, will you?"

Inga did as she asked, while grumbling, "It still seems ridiculous to me that you're having to dress for a social event when we're surrounded by military tents and army officers."

"It may look like a party from the outside, but Lord Audley's salons are more of a hotbed of information and opinions than anything else."

Inga's head snapped up. "He's held these before?"

"One every three to four months, give or take. He announces the dates with little notice to keep the huns from turning them into target practice for their aeroplanes. Lucien went a time or two and told me about them, so I know what to expect."

"And that is..."

"Lord Audley proposes a question for debate and watches carefully to see where the opinions of his guests land. Only his lordship knows what else he gathers from the events. For example, tonight he expects Rex to subtly question Major Edgewell. I'll watch the two of them, and everyone else. With any luck, someone will slip up and give us a hint of where we can find our traitor."

"Rex knows about you?"

Dora shook her head. "Oh no, absolutely not. And I intend to keep my distance from him. I doubt he'd welcome my involvement."

"I imagine not." Inga sat back and watched as Dora finished buttoning her shirt. "At least let me do something with your hair."

Dora let Inga mother her for as long as she could stand it, and then said her goodbyes. For once, she left through the front door rather than her bedroom window, and climbed into the motor car waiting out front. The soldier assigned to drive her to the event navigated the streets of Le Touquet in silence, both of them enjoying the cool breeze coming through the open windows.

Light poured from the windows of Lord Audley's modest rented accommodation, offering passersby glimpses of the people milling inside. Sergeant Grimsby opened the door when Dora knocked and motioned her into the sitting room.

Dora was one of the last to arrive. She counted at least twenty others, mostly men, but not entirely. The furniture had been pushed aside to make room for everyone to mill around between the sitting and dining rooms. Two junior officers circulated holding trays of drinks and small canapes.

Dora's practiced eye skimmed the faces of the other guests, her mind automatically slotting them into categories — officer, titled, wealthy, wife. She supposed she should add a new category, if for no one but herself.

Widow.

It felt incredibly dishonest to use that word to describe herself, given the length of her marriage, not to mention the false pretence of it. She'd be quick enough to lay claim to the freedoms it would offer her post-war, but here and now, she hesitated to use it.

She slid between pockets of people, making her way to Lord Audley, where he stood in the back of the room. She kept a demure smile on her face as she thanked him for the invitation. He replied with the required welcome and she took her leave, claiming to see someone else.

The person she'd spotted was Lord Rex. Dora helped herself to a glass of wine and eased into position behind two tall men in a heated discussion about gun oils. How anyone could get so excited about cleaning their weapons was beyond Dora, but she pasted a smile on her face and pretended to be interested.

Rex took no note of her. He was standing with a trio of young men, all in their twenties, if she had to guess. Their faces were tanned, their uniforms brushed and pressed. Only the sling wrapped around Rex's shoulder set him apart from the others.

Rex said something that made the other men throw back their heads and chortle in glee. He basked in their delight at his cleverness. He was likely accustomed to being the centre of attention, as the son of an earl. Dora was fairly certain he was the second son, but given the speed with which heirs fell in battle, she couldn't be sure this was still true.

Was he handsome? The woman standing nearby seemed to think so, if the hungry look in her eyes was any clue. Dora assured herself that any assessments of his appearance were merely clinical, and not out of any appreciation of his wide shoulders, narrow waist, and chiselled cheekbones.

"Captain Bankes-Fernsby seems to be recovering well," a voice remarked from Dora's side.

Dora turned to find Theresa Edgewell standing next to her, eyeing Rex above the rim of her wineglass.

"I was terribly worried I'd have to write to his mother, but finally his fever broke..." Mrs Edgewell's voice trailed off into a whispered prayer of thanks to the heavens above.

"He seems hale enough now, Mrs Edgewell," Dora reassured her. "I believe you can firmly set your pen aside. You look lovely this evening. Have you done something different with your hair?"

Theresa Edgewell patted her hair self-consciously. She was over a decade younger than her distinguished husband, which would put her in her late thirties. Their lack of children hadn't impacted their commitment to one another. When the major declared his intention to go to war, Mrs Edgewell had gone right along with him.

It was an unusual situation, but it made sense when you took Major Edgewell's disability into account. He'd sustained an injury in the Boer War and relied on a cane to get around. He was permanently assigned to a desk job in the command post, while his wife kept watch over the nurses in the medical corps. What modern medicine couldn't heal, Mrs Edgewell attempted to pray away.

"I did the best I could with what the Lord gave me, Lady Dorothy," Mrs Edgewell responded. "You look lovely as well."

Niceties exchanged, the women suffered through a stilted conversation until Lord Audley cleared his throat and coughed a few times to get everyone's attention.

"Welcome to you all. Tonight, I've invited you for another, hopefully lively, discussion. As always, I ask that we respect differences of opinion. None here are enemies. Those lie some fifty miles away, deep in the trenches. Spirited discourse is encouraged, so long as we can all walk away as friends at the end of the night." Lord Audley scanned the room, making sure everyone understood. "You left your rank and title at the door when you came inside. Here, you may speak freely, so that we may all learn from one another. Is that understood?"

Murmurs of agreement sounded. Everyone was eager to know what the topic for debate would be.

"My question for the evening is one which has led to raised voices throughout Westminster. Should the government send more troops to our shores? While I know we would all welcome the arrival of more reserves, we also know better than anyone else what horrors these new soldiers will face. Additionally, these extra resources will come at a price. Factories and farmlands will be emptied by any new calls to arms. So what say you, my guests? Shall the government send more troops or are we better off using those under our guidance as wisely as we can? Believe me when I say there is no simple answer. The floor is yours."

Dora had to hand it to Lord Audley. The question was one on everyone's lips, and all here would have an opinion. It was a senior officer who stepped forward first, declaring his support for only a modest increase.

One of Rex's friends spoke next, recounting the challenges of holding the line with too few men. "Begging your pardon, sir, but the dead can't hold a gun."

Dora had plenty of thoughts on the topic, but she kept them all to herself. This wasn't a forum for her to stun everyone with her brilliant insights. Someday, that might be different, but for now, she was firmly in the role of observer.

She was caught off guard when Theresa Edgewell dared to speak up.

"I know many of you will think me unqualified to participate, but the spirit compels me to use my voice. It is true there are more men in England who could be ferried to our aid. It is also true that we need all the help we can get, especially after the losses we've seen this year. Our hospitals are still full of men, and women such as myself and Lady Dorothy can only do so much to ease their pain. Thus, my heart calls for me to remind you of a third group, which none so far have mentioned tonight."

Major Edgewell had his jaw clenched, as though he didn't trust himself to speak. While Dora wondered who Theresa meant, Lord Audley asked her to continue.

"The prisoners of war. Many a good man lies behind enemy lines, waiting for us to free them from their shackles and chains. If we need fresh support, we should be concentrating our efforts on rescuing those soldiers who are held captive."

"That's a fool's errand," Major Edgewell blurted.

Mrs Edgewell's cheeks burned, but she didn't hold back.

"Perhaps it is, but you cannot convince me that it isn't worth the effort. My brother sits behind those lines, and has done so for nearly a year. Can you imagine how much he must have learned by now about their strengths and weaknesses? If not released by rescue, why not negotiation? We must bring our men back home, no matter where they are."

"I agree with you," her husband said before anyone else could intervene. "You know I want Roland to come home safe as much as you do. This is why we need more men and need them now. We ask our allies to fill our ranks and expect the Yanks to work miracles. Our enemy is exhausted. We should press any advantage we have and crush them before the year is out."

A few 'hear, hears' echoed from around the room. The discussion turned again as another man offered his thoughts on the matter.

Dora watched the faces of those around her while weighing her task. Lord Audley had been clear with her. Only he, his soldier-servant, and the major knew of Lucien's orders.

Dora had heard enough of Rex's conversation with Sergeant Grimsby to doubt his involvement. From what the man had said at dinner, everyone he loved was back in England. Lord Audley was his ticket to a better life, not to mention insuring he survived long enough to benefit from the connection.

That left two — Major Edgewell and Lord Audley. Dora forced herself to view Lord Audley as a suspect. Her father detested the man and had for years. She put herself in her father's shoes and judged Lord Audley as he would.

Her father would frown and tell her she was well off the mark. Lord Audley was a thorn in his side because he was a leader of the opposition, not because he was a traitor. Dora could no more believe he'd help the enemy than she could imagine her own father doing so.

That left one — Major Edgewell. She hardly knew the man,

but she was familiar enough with his wife to have a sense of what he valued. Hard work, respect for the almighty, and the homeland.

On any other day, she'd draw a line through his name as well. But tonight's discussion had been enlightening. Major Edgewell had a weakness. His brother-in-law was in enemy hands. What would he do to ensure his continued existence?

Dora didn't need to look any further than her own family to know how far one would go to save their nearest and dearest. Would her mother trade another man's life to save hers?

Her mind balked at the question. Maybe... but then again, her mother wasn't so callous that she'd sign someone's death warrant and then sleep peacefully that night.

She wished she could question the major. A dozen angles came to mind. Would Rex think of them as well? She hated that she was dependent on him doing the upfront work to pry into their chief suspect's mind.

Unfortunately, Major Edgewell didn't provide either Dora or Rex with an opportunity to engage with him. As soon as Lord Audley called the debate to a close, he claimed he needed to get his wife home and departed without a backward glance.

Dora added his hasty exit to her tally of questionable behaviours and soon after, brought her own evening to an end. She wanted to talk things over with the only person left here whom she trusted unconditionally — her friend Inga.

Chapter 9
Checkmate Marks The Start

The two women sat on either end of the narrow bed with a wooden chessboard occupying the space between them. The window was open to allow in what little breeze there was. Half a dozen birch and mahogany carved game pieces lay forgotten on the side, casualties of a battle of wits.

Inga's hand hovered over a pawn before shifting sideways to move her knight instead. Her brow relaxed, and she blinked away the last of her tension. She'd managed to shore up her defences before Dora noticed the opening she'd left with a prior ill-thought move.

Inga's satisfaction, however, was short-lived. When she glanced upward to see what was taking Dora so long to make her own move, she found the young woman staring off into space.

"If you've got somewhere else to be, don't let our chess date stop you from going," Inga said.

Dora blinked a few times, coming back to the present. "What? Oh sorry, I didn't realise it was my move."

"Not only that, but you've overlooked the fact you've

checked me three times. Not to seem ungrateful, but the game is generally more fun when one's opponent puts forth a minimum of effort."

Dora blushed under her friend's chiding. "I'm rubbish this evening. Please accept my sincere apologies for my poor showing."

Inga brushed the apology aside. "I meant what I said earlier. If you have sleuthing to do, then go. I won't take it too hard."

"If I had an idea of where to go next, I would. Unfortunately, after spending a full day of muddling through ideas, I'm no closer to reaching a decision."

"Will it help to talk things out?"

"That's all I've done since I left Lord Audley's home last night. Granted, the conversations have been entirely with myself, but the problem remains. Even though I have a suspicion Major Edgewell is our man, I have no way of proving it."

Inga leaned against the pillow resting against the metal headboard and surveyed her friend. Dark shadows marred Dora's English rose complexion. Her hair was still wet from washing it in the basin, the ends leaving damp patches on her lightweight shift. Her lips were pulled so tight, they were tinged blue. Grief, stress, and the ticking timepiece hanging over her like the sword of Damocles demanded a heavy toll.

Still, there had to be some way to help Dora. Inga's gaze fell onto the chessboard. Without asking, she fluttered her hands above the board, moving the pieces back to their starting positions.

"Let's try approaching this from a fresh angle. Instead of getting bogged down in the specifics of each individual, let's look at the whole." Inga motioned to the first row of chess pieces. "For the sake of discussion, Lord Audley will be our king. Major Edgewell can be queen, given he is second in command. The sergeant is a rook, Lord Rex a knight, and the remaining men under Audley's command are the pawns. Fair enough?"

Dora nodded, her curiosity inflamed by Inga's unusual approach.

"What's the first thing you notice when you look at the board?"

"The opponent?" Dora asked, her voice wavering.

"Yes, exactly. There is very likely a similar command structure on the other side, and many pieces in play. Our traitor might be an important piece, but they are far from alone."

Dora crossed her legs and sat up straight, giving Inga her full attention. "I can already feel the gears in my mind spluttering into motion. Keep going."

"The next step is to start the game itself. There's nothing stopping you from using a knight in the opening move, but we both know it is far more common to use a pawn. What does that tell you?"

Dora's brow furrowed as she stared at the board, her focus elsewhere. Instead of seeing the hand-carved pieces, she pictured train tracks and wagons filled with young recruits. The battles in the spring had exacted an incredible toll on the allied forces, but it wasn't the lost lives that came to Dora's mind. Instead, she tallied the number of complaints she'd overheard about supplies going missing, scouts never coming back, and roads and bridges destroyed.

She'd been so focused on the latest skirmish, she'd lost sight of the real game. Every move was a calculated risk, but experts at the game always thought several moves ahead.

"We've had a traitor in our midst for a while now," Dora said with utter confidence. When Inga raised her eyebrows in a silent question, Dora added more. "They've leaked information on troop movements and supply lines. That's how the Huns knew which areas were the weakest."

"Just one?" Inga asked, trailing her finger in front of the line of pawns.

"Of course not. In fact, I'm sure both sides have spies stationed any and everywhere they can. This is why Lord Audley is here, instead of being closer to the front. He oversees the men who are acting as eyes and ears. I'd half suspected it, but after seeing his non-reaction to me showing up in his home, I'm sure of it. Who else would be so collected when finding a stranger in their study?"

"Where does Major Edgewell fit into this? Or Sergeant Grimsby?"

"Aside from the king, the rook and queen are the most important pieces on the board. It's why Audley is so hesitant to believe them responsible. No smart king would elevate someone to those positions without trusting them inherently. If either of them are a spy, it reflects as much on Audley as on themselves."

"And yet, you believe Major Edgewell is responsible for Lucien's death. Why?"

Dora had a ready answer. "He has a weakness. His brother-in-law is in enemy hands. That gives the enemy leverage."

"It does," Inga agreed. "And yet, Lord Audley hasn't isolated the major, nor even hinted that he might have gone rogue. What makes you think you know better than the master himself?"

Dora was stumped by that question. Inga snorted a laugh when Dora huffed in frustration.

"I thought you were going to help me, Inga! Instead, you've removed the only viable suspect I had."

"How can you say that?" Inga countered. "Look at the board, Dora. Lord Audley said only three men knew Lucien's travel plans. What about all these other pieces? Could someone have eavesdropped?"

"Doubtful, since he has a corner office on the top floor. The building is heavily guarded. Even I would think twice before attempting to sneak in."

"And yet, you made it into his study, with plenty of time to search through his personal papers, had you so chosen. Why not the same for Major Edgewell? Have you looked into their domestics? You know how often the upper class forgets servants are in the room."

Dora rocked backward when Inga exposed her blind spot. She frowned, completely disappointed at herself. With a deft hand, she plucked several pieces from the game board and began dividing them into two groups.

"This is Lord Audley's household," Dora explained. Hearing the words out loud was as much for Inga's benefit as her own. "There's Audley himself, the sergeant, and his housekeeper. The housekeeper is an old English girl, been here since the turn of the century. She depends on English tourists to keep her afloat. I can't imagine the war is any help to her, nor would a loss be."

"What's the other pile?"

"This is the Major's household. This time, he's the king and his wife Theresa is the queen. These pawns are the cook, the maid, and the soldier-servant acting as valet for the major. More ears to hear, as you'd say."

"What do you think about your suspect pool now?" Inga asked. "Do you still share Lord Audley's confidence that only three people could have known about the mission?"

"I wasn't exactly confident before," Dora pointed out, giving Inga a sideways glance. She examined the pieces laying before her, picking them up one by one. "We've got a major, a wife, and three servants. How in God's creation am I going to investigate them all, especially given my limited hours of free time?"

"You could always ask Rex for help."

Dora answered Inga's comment with a glare. However, as much as Dora disliked the idea of teaming up with Rex, especially given Lord Audley's order to keep to herself, she needed assistance.

She dropped the chess pieces onto the bed and wiped her hands over her face in exasperation. Then her gaze landed on the obvious solution.

"You could help me."

Inga inclined her head in her most regal bearing. "I could be persuaded."

Dora chuckled at her friend's reply. Persuaded? Chances are Inga was as keen to get involved as Dora herself.

"I know how we could knock out three people with one go. But you'll have to accompany me on a visit to the place you like least in Le Touquet."

Inga arched an eyebrow. "The laundry hall?"

"Worse. Major Edgewell's home. We can pay a call on Mrs Edgewell. If we play our cards right, I'm sure we can come up with an excuse to leave her parlour and snoop around. Maybe even speak with the servants."

Inga didn't hide her disgust. She really did not get on with Mrs Edgewell. This was fast becoming a true test of the limits of their friendship. "I suppose I can hold my nose for a couple of hours, given the critical nature of the situation."

Dora clapped her hands in delight, eliciting a glare from Inga, who never approved of her shows of enthusiasm, even when limited to the privacy of their shared quarters. That was one of the reasons why Dora still did them.

Inga's glare shifted into a stern gaze. She fixed her brown eyes on Dora's emerald ones, immune to her feminine charms.

"Very well, Viscountess Clever Cat. What will be the pretext for our visit? This isn't exactly a town where one spends the afternoon making social calls."

Once again, Dora had no ready answer. This time, however, she had hope. It was like engine oil for her cunning mind. Much more quickly than before, she arrived at a solution.

"You are right, dear Inga, that a social visit would raise far too many eyebrows. But if I recall correctly, Mrs Edgewell has always said that her door is open to anyone who needs spiritual guidance."

Inga waved her hands, desperately begging her friend to stop that train of thought before it left the station.

Dora ignored her and blithely continued. "Like you, I have no desire to submit myself to hours of Old Testament tales. Therefore, I'll have to make it clear that my problem is more worldly, and not a weakness of the spirit. Lucky for us both, I happen to have a question weighing on my mind."

Inga was intrigued. She motioned for Dora to get on with it.

"My mother demands my return, but my patriotic nature calls me to remain. I wonder if Theresa Edgewell has any guidance for balancing familial obligations with love for the homeland."

Inga tipped an imaginary hat in Dora's direction. "That's fine enough for you, but what am I meant to do while this conversation takes place? She's hardly going to take you into her confidence with me sitting at your side."

"As Julius Caesar said, divide et impera."

Inga's mouth flattened. "Divide and conquer? If you're matching wits with Saint Theresa, I take it that I'm getting the hired help."

"Do you want to swap roles?"

"To answer that, I will offer a Caesar quote of my own," Inga said. "*I am prepared to resort to anything, to submit to anything, for the sake of the commonwealth...* Anything, that is, except spending time with Theresa Edgewell. If the hired help are half as annoyed by her as I am, I'm sure I'll have little trouble convincing them to tell me about all the dirt they've been dusting under the carpet."

Chapter 10
Leave No Man (Or Cat) Behind

As a soldier at the front, Rex had a number of concerns on his mind at any given time. Right then, there were two keeping him up at night. The first was the identity of the traitor in their midst.

He'd exhausted all avenues for investigation on that front and had reached a conclusion. Major Edgewell had sold them out. There was no other answer that made sense.

That left Rex free to focus on his other matter.

Mews.

The kitten had disappeared from his room during the night, leaping out the window he'd left open. Normally, the kitten was back in his bed when he awoke. But so far, there'd been no sign of him.

Rex checked his watch, confirming he had a little time before his early evening meeting with Lord Audley. He shoved his feet into his boots, for the first time cursing the lack of a kitten chasing after his laces. Never mind that the feline was more feral than domesticated. Rex had grown to have fond feelings for the little chap.

Outside his lodgings, Rex surveyed the late evening

landscape, searching for any hint of a marmalade tail. "Mews! Mews!" he called, clicking his tongue. He must look utterly ridiculous to anyone passing by. How would he even explain what he was doing? Perhaps he was better off letting the cat go.

Decision made, he turned around, took three steps along the pavement, before darting down the narrow alley that ran alongside his lodgings.

He couldn't leave the cat. He couldn't explain why, but in his heart he knew there was no choice but to carry on with his search.

At the other end of the alley stood a boulangerie. Every morning, the buttery, rich smell of freshly baked croissants perfumed the air. It would certainly be attractive to a cat. Rex started there, giving a sharp rap on the half-open rear door.

"Pardon me, but did you happen to see an orange tabby kitten today?"

A heavyset man in a white apron looked up from the dough he was kneading to glare at the man who dared to interrupt him with such a silly question.

"It was in my bin this morning, dreadful thing," he said in a thick French accent. "I shooed it away."

Rex's heart sank. "Which way? Which direction did the cat run?" He stood firm, making it clear he wasn't leaving until he got an answer.

The baker pointed toward the front of his shop. "It went to the street."

Rex didn't know what made him madder — the fact that the baker had run the kitten off, or that he hadn't even thought to nudge it away from the direction of the busy street.

There were no other hiding places between the doorway where he stood and the busy road. Rex walked ahead, his hopes of finding the cat safe dwindling with every step. He mentally steeled himself for what he might find. That particular street was always busy with cars, horses, and other vehicles, all ferrying supplies from one waypoint to another. Nonetheless, he was determined to find out what had happened to the cat.

At the end of the alleyway, he glanced left and right along the street. There were no signs of the cat on either the cobblestones or the walkways. Rex was left to guess which way the cat was most likely to have gone. With the baker chasing after him, Mews probably hadn't gone left, toward the main entrance of the boulangerie. So, Rex looked to his right where he saw a wide open doorway.

Jackpot.

The doorway turned out to be an entry into a cavernous warehouse overflowing with crates of various sizes. There were plenty of nooks and crannies where a scared kitten might decide to hide.

Rex checked his watch, dismayed at how quickly the time was passing. Those few extra minutes he had were quickly dwindling down to none. He knew he should turn back if he wanted to make it to his meeting on time.

He reminded himself that he could come back later, but his heart refused to follow his head. What if the kitten was trapped, or worse yet, injured?

Rex walked through the doorway. He saw a couple of men in uniform stacking crates and made his way over to them.

The shorter man of the pair came to attention and offered a brief salute. "Hello, Captain. Can I help you with something?"

"Err, yes," he replied, wondering how to phrase his question. Best to be frank. "You haven't by any chance seen a small kitten?"

"Orange one, about this big?" the other man replied, holding his hands apart to indicate the right size.

"Yes, that's the one!" Rex answered, hardly daring to believe his luck.

"I saw him scampering around between the crates earlier, chasing after a fly. Cute little bugger. You might try further back. We've been moving things around and he might have got stuck."

"I'll do just that," Rex answered, thanking the men and then letting them get back to their work. He followed the direction that the man had indicated, weaving between crates stacked taller than he was.

It was a veritable mountain of supplies; the labels indicating everything from cloth uniforms to bullets to bandages. All the items were destined to end up at the front, each critical to the war effort.

Rex took great care not to bump against anything, imagining the domino effect that would happen if even one crate came tumbling down in the tightly packed warehouse.

"Mews! Mews!" he called, clicking his tongue again. "Mews, are you there?" He stood stock still and listened carefully. Nothing. He tried again, his voice more forceful. "Mews, it's me. Do you want a treat?" he added.

This time, he was rewarded with a barely audible miaow.

Rex didn't think about what would happen if someone saw him or heard him talking to the cat. He was so excited to hear any sign of life that he darted around a box, setting aside his previous care. The miaows grew louder as he hurried along the walkway until finally he located their source. From between a stack of crates peered out a pair of yellow eyes.

"Mews!" he cooed. "You're here! You're safe."

The poor cat gave a plaintive miaow, desperate for rescue. Rex sized up the situation, determining how best to free the feline. He shifted the shortest stack of crates ever so carefully, only a centimetre at a time, wiggling them just wide enough to make a space for the little kitten to come crawling out.

The poor beast was hunched into a tiny puff ball. Rex

dropped to his knees and reached his hand into the space to coax the scared cat out. As soon as Mews was free, Rex tucked the cat tight into the crook of his injured arm, stroking its forehead with his finger. "Mews, I was so worried about you. Thank goodness I found you."

Before he could rise, Rex heard a gruff voice call a warning. "You there! What are you doing?"

Rex straightened up hurriedly, balancing the cat in his sling, and turned around to reassure whoever it was that he wasn't up to no good.

It was a fellow officer coming down the aisle towards him. The officer's grim expression softened only a little when he spotted the small kitten in Rex's arm.

"Sorry about that, Captain. We've had some problems in the warehouse and I've been keeping an eye out to see if anyone's been sneaking around. When I saw you hunched over like that, I assumed the worst."

"No problem," Rex replied. "It was an easy mistake to make, especially since I'm not meant to be here. I'd appreciate it if you didn't mention this episode to anyone else. I'm not sure whether rescuing kittens is allowed, given I'm still on medical leave."

The other officer snorted and mimed turning a blind eye to the whole matter.

Rex turned to leave, but then the rest of what the man said sank in. He spun back, halting the man before he got too far away. "What did you mean when you said that there were problems with supplies?"

"We've had crates of bullets go missing, clothing and food damaged beyond use. I don't know who it is and I can't imagine why they would want to do such a thing. Anyone with half a mind can see how important these items are." He lowered his voice to a growl and added, "When I find them, you can be sure I'll be sending them off for the appropriate punishment." He sliced a finger across his throat, leaving no question as to what he meant.

Rex shivered and was thankful that he was wearing his uniform with his insignias. Imagine if he'd been mistaken for some sort of enemy spy. The excuse of a missing cat might not have been enough to save him from a night in the stocks, or worse.

Rex asked a few more questions, intent on gathering information. It was only the ringing of the church bells that reminded him of his original appointment. He looked at his watch again and was horrified to see that the time for his meeting with Lord Audley had arrived. Here he was, standing in a warehouse at least a 10-minute walk from Audley's office, with a kitten in his arm no less.

He kept a tight grip on the kitten as he ran up the alleyway, ignoring the angry shout of the baker who had once again been disturbed. Rex aimed straight for his bedroom window, which was thankfully still propped open. He stuck his hand inside, letting the cat fall onto the bed, and then eased the window down until only a small crack remained. At least this time, the cat was sure to be there when he returned.

His mind much at ease, he hurried as quickly as he could to Lord Audley's office in the Hotel de Ville. His arm throbbed with each of his pounding steps along the pavement. The upside to the pain was it focused him on the upcoming conversation. Sweat drenched his brow and his uniform had a terrible crease running across the middle by the time he got there.

There was no helping it.

"Captain Bankes-Fernsby here to see Lord Audley. Sorry, I'm late."

Sergeant Grimsby took in his dishevelled state and shook his head. "He won't be happy. I hope you've got a good excuse for your tardiness and the way you look."

Sergeant Grimsby handed Rex a handkerchief to wipe off his face before rapping on his lordship's door. Lord Audley was indeed not pleased to see Rex when he came through his office door.

"I sincerely hope that you have an explanation for why you've been so disrespectful of my time, Captain Bankes-Fernsby."

Rex's feet hadn't been the only thing that had been moving quickly. During his mad dash across looked Le Touquet, he realised that he might yet have a way of gathering proof they had a traitor.

He sat in the chair across from Lord Audley, smoothing the wrinkle in his shirt to give himself a moment for his heart rate to slow down to a more normal pace. He had come up with a plan, but it would require a small amount of fibbing. Rex suspected that Lord Audley was the type of man to appreciate such liberties rather than frown upon them.

Therefore, it was with little hesitation that he looked Lord Audley in the eyes and declared, "I know the identity of our traitor."

Lord Audley's eyebrows shot up. "You have proof?"

"Circumstantial, for now," Rex replied. "That's why I was late. I was looking into another avenue for identifying our traitor. Given the importance of the individual in question, I knew that you would need proof."

"Who is it?"

This was the critical juncture of the meeting. Rex kept his voice steady as he answered, "I'd prefer not to say until I have evidence beyond a shadow of a doubt of their complicity."

Lord Audley sat forward in his chair and rested his forearms on the edge of his desk. "Do you have a plan to gather this evidence?"

Rex explained about his trip to the warehouse, leaving out all mention of the mischievous kitten. He told about the supply shortages and the fact that someone was clearly doing their best to sabotage the troops from the inside.

"Either the traitor is doing more damage than sabotaging missions, or we have two people working against us. Regardless, I can't imagine these instances aren't somehow related. I plan to investigate the theft and damage in the warehouse to see if I can find a connection. With a little time, I'll have evidence you can use to ensure that justice is served."

Rex held perfectly still, sweat still trickling along his spine, while he waited for Lord Audley's reaction. The clock on the wall ticking away the seconds was the only sound. His lordship's face gave no hint as to the thoughts that were going on behind his eyes.

Rex felt his muscles tense as his nerves grew taut. Had he made a mistake in speaking through so many vagaries instead of plainly stating his suspicions? Rex was dependent on Lord Audley's blessing to continue with this avenue of investigation. His superior would be well within his rights to demand the name of the individual in question or detailed outlines of his plans.

However, Lord Audley did nothing of the sort. He met Rex's gaze, taking his measure. Rex didn't dare even blink. "Good work, Captain. You moved faster than I would have expected. And you're right thinking we'll need evidence. I'm willing to give you a few days, but no more than that... not with so much at stake. As before, tell no one else what you're working upon and report only to me."

Rex sensed the dismissal in Lord Audley's words and

hurried to rise from the chair. He wanted to get out of the room before Audley had second thoughts.

"Oh, Rex," Lord Audley called just as the captain reached the threshold of his office.

Rex turned around and braced himself.

"Next time we have an appointment, make sure you're on time."

Rex gave no hint of the relief he felt at that small admonishment. It could have been so much worse.

"Yes sir, understood, sir."

And with that, he left.

Chapter 11

The Moral Quandary

Dora glanced at her friend's face as they walked beneath a gas lamp. What she saw was enough to make her grab onto Inga's arm and pull her to a stop.

"I know you're girding your loins, but could you keep some of the angst from your countenance?"

Inga turned the full weight of her glower onto Dora.

Dora was unmoved. "Come on then, chin up. Pretend we're off to tea at the Savoy."

"Fine chance of that," Inga grumbled. She did, however, adjust her expression into something vaguely pleasant. It was as good as it was going to get, so Dora let her off with a grateful smile.

Mrs Edgewell had been happy enough to acquiesce to Dora's request for a private meeting. It so happened that the Major was occupied that very evening, leaving his wife free to entertain. Dora had left off mentioning that Inga would accompany her for fear of being shown the figurative door instead of welcomed in.

A medieval cardinal by the name of Barberini once advised the duchess of Modena that it was less difficult to ask forgiveness for something done than to ask permission for doing it. When Dora had read that fact, she'd taken the guidance to heart. Thus, Dora was certain Mrs Edgewell's fine manners would demand she accept Inga's presence as a fait accompli.

The Edgewells had commandeered a larger home in a prime location in the centre of Le Touquet. It wasn't particularly wide, but it had a neat front garden turned vegetable patch and three floors of living space. Expansive front windows were designed to make the most of the coastal sunlight in the public rooms. Heavy shutters blocked the bedroom windows from prying eyes. The dormer windows providing living space for the servants.

It was the maid who answered the door. She was young, perhaps even younger than Dora, with mousy brown hair pulled into a tight bun that was barely visible under her white cap. She moved like a skittish colt, bobbing her head as she told the women to come in. After taking their hats, the maid showed them into a modest parlour where Theresa Edgewell sat waiting.

Mrs Edgewell rose from her seat, her mouth slipping open when she saw Inga come striding in behind Dora. She recovered quickly enough. "Hello, Lady Dorothy. Pardon my surprise. I wasn't expecting you to bring someone else."

Inga looked like she'd swallowed a lemon as she apologised. "I didn't want Dora to be out wandering the streets on her own after dark. I know she wishes to speak in private, so I thought I might avail myself of the chance to learn something of my own. Would it be a terrible imposition if I asked on your cook for the recipe for the shortbread you served at the picnic? I'm happy enough to wait in the kitchen until your tête-à-tête is done."

"I suppose that's all right," Mrs Edgewell demurred. "Why don't you sit and I'll send Tilly to ask whether she's available?"

Mrs Edgewell shifted her attention to the maid. "Tilly, please bring us a pot of tea and a selection of Cook's latest treats."

The maid left to do her mistress's bidding, leaving the three society ladies shifting uncomfortably in the silence that remained.

The room was comfortably furnished and clearly much used. The fabrics didn't coordinate perfectly, despite their good quality. Dora suspected Mrs Edgewell had bought the items here, acquiring them over the several years she'd been stationed in Le Touquet. A leather-bound hardback sat on a side table, a bookmark sticking out midway through. The angle was wrong for Dora to see the title, but she guessed it more likely belonged to the Major than his wife. Theresa Edgewell needed only one book. When she wasn't studying the scripture, she kept herself entertained with the basket of knitting beside her armchair.

Dora didn't know anything about knitting, so she opted for another safe topic of conversation. "It's been nice to have a few days of sunshine."

"Yes, and the picnic was a lovely idea. It was yours, Mrs Edgewell? Rather ingenious of you to suggest," Inga said, not even needing to lie. Staying far away from where Mrs Edgewell held court had ensured Inga had a perfectly fine time at the event.

The conversation remained within the confines of polite inanities until Tilly returned with a steaming teapot, three cups and saucers, and a small plate of biscuits.

"Cook said she can spare a few minutes," Tilly said, after setting the tray onto the coffee table.

"If you don't mind, I'll take my tea in the kitchen," Inga said, rising from her chair. She beat a hasty retreat, leaving Dora with her prey.

Mrs Edgewell sat upright, her posture solid enough to balance a book on her head. The starched collar of her blouse buttoned up to her chin, despite the wave of warm summer weather. She smiled benevolently, blithely unaware that she was sitting in the hot seat. She laid her hands on her lap, leaned forward, and said, "You mentioned you needed advice. I can't promise to hold the answers, but mayhap the divine will grant me guidance on how best to help you. Anything you say, I promise to keep in confidence. Come now, tell me what's on your mind."

Dora had mastered control over her facial expressions by the age of five when she'd learnt to cry on command. She let her lower lip tremble for a moment while pretending to gather her courage.

"Thank you, Mrs — may I call you Theresa?"

"Of course you may."

Dora let her shoulders relax. "Thank you, and please, call me Dorothy. It will make me feel as though I've come to a friend for help, rather than my superior in the ward."

Theresa smiled, clearly thrilled to be on a first name basis with a member of the upper echelons of British society.

"The death of my darling Lucien has left me bereft. My mother insists I come to mourn properly, but how can I abandon our wounded in their hour of need? I'm so torn. I have no idea what to do."

Theresa batted her lashes as she considered Dora's quandary. "My, that is a difficult choice. I can see why this decision pains you."

"It is a question with no right answer, or none as far as I can see," Dora admitted. "There's more to consider than just my feelings. My brother was among the fallen at the Somme. I know my mother wants me to come home as much for my needs as for her own."

"Then you must go to her, Dorothy."

"Really?" Dora's eyes widened like a doe. "But what of my responsibilities here?"

"In this matter, our Lord Father is clear." Theresa pulled a pocket-sized bible from between her cushion and armrest and showed it to Dora before returning it to its place. "First Timothy, chapter five, verse eight says that anyone who does not provide for their relatives has denied the faith and is worse than an unbeliever. Family comes first, above all else."

Dora released an exaggerated sigh, smiling as though a weight had been lifted from her shoulders. "Is this why you are here, Theresa? Apologies if I seem impertinent. I couldn't help but hear your impassioned pleas to save your brother when we were guests of Lord Audley. It must pain you terribly to live with the unknowns of his captivity."

"He is alive, and that is knowledge enough for me now." Theresa's glance slipped sideways and a flicker of discomfort passed across her face. "To answer your question, yes. I know my presence here benefits my brother... and the other men held with him," she hastened to add. "Life doesn't always make our choices easy, but I trust in the Above to guide my hand."

"I suppose you are right, but I can't help feeling that I'm failing our men here who are so bravely giving their lives on the front line."

"We can't save them all, Dorothy. They know this as well. We must find a way to be at peace with our decisions." Theresa picked up her cup and sipped her tea. "When will you go? We'll need to rearrange the schedules until I can get another nurse sent our way."

Dora gently raised and lowered her shoulders. "I'll have to speak to Lord Audley about the arrangements. With the Germans and their submarines, his lordship will know best when and how it will be safest for me to get across the Channel."

"I'll pray for a safe journey."

Dora was spared any further discussions by Inga's return. "Did you get your recipe?" she asked when Inga came through the parlour doorway.

Inga patted her pocket. "That one and a few more. Your cook is wise beyond her ways, Mrs Edgewell. I've no doubt her advice will help my cook back in England master the perfect shortbread biscuit."

Dora and Inga took their leave, thanking Mrs Edgewell for her time and wise advice on their way out. Arm in arm, they walked along the edge of the cobblestone street until they were out of eyesight.

"What did you find out?" Dora asked, unable to wait until they were back in their lodgings.

"The Edgewells pay decent wages, but the cook and maid would prefer to spend their day off in a place of their own choosing, rather than in the church sanctuary. Major Edgewell's man keeps to himself, which is fine by them. Neither showed any fondness for the gent, and both were happy enough that he spends his free evenings elsewhere. What of yourself?" Inga asked.

"I think our sainted Theresa might be wearing a bent halo. Her priorities are clear. Family above all else. If anyone could be convinced to betray her homeland, it's her. She'd do anything to save her brother. Anything at all."

Inga shook her head. "I'd love that to be true, but there's a cavernous gap between knowing and proving."

"That's why I'm going out again tonight. Major Edgewell won't be back for hours. He's off playing cards with the other senior officers. That leaves me a window of time when I can sneak in after Theresa, her cook, and maid turn in."

Inga's grimace showed her feelings better than any words.

"I don't need to search the whole house. Unless I'm wildly

wrong, and I rarely am, if Theresa is hiding anything, it can only be in one of two places — her knitting basket or her bible."

"Check that writing desk I saw tucked into the corner," Inga said. "I noticed the key was missing from the lock."

"Good thing I've got lock picks, and my borrowed uniform has plenty of pockets. If I find anything, I'll take it straight to Lord Audley. We should hurry. I'd like to get all my visits done and still have time to sleep before our shift starts tomorrow morning."

Inga and Dora walked home as fast as their skirts would allow.

Chapter 12
The Whispered Prayer

Dora retraced her steps, moving much more quickly now that she was in trousers and boots. She veered down a side street and crept into the Edgewell's courtyard.

The courtyard was on the south side of the house, with several shade trees in full bloom. Dora waited for a cloud to pass over the moon before slipping out of the shadows under the heavy branches. She dashed to the kitchen window, keeping low. She raised her head to peek through, ensuring the dark room was empty before picking the flimsy lock on the back door.

She took off her boots and left them sitting by the kitchen door. Although she'd stuffed the toes with cloth, there was no getting around the fact that they were too large. She didn't want them slipping from her heel and banging against the wooden floors at an inopportune time.

A gas lamp flickered, casting strange shadows across the hallway. Dora stilled, listening carefully. The only creaks came from overhead. The kitchen had been spotless and the rest of the house was dark. Everyone at home had gone to bed. That left the ground floor free for her to explore.

She checked the time on the wall clock and judged her

window to be at least an hour. She had time to be thorough. Although the parlour was her primary destination, she opted for the room overlooking the courtyard. The door was ajar. Dora nudged it, allowing light from the hall to illuminate the room's contents.

A practical wooden desk and leather chair sat in one corner, framed by two walls lined with books. This must be the Major's study. Dora closed the door behind her, holding the handle so it wouldn't make a noise. The drapes were still open, allowing in enough moonlit to facilitate her search. If she found any papers, she'd take them to the window to read.

Dora didn't expect to find anything of note. Therefore, she wasn't disappointed when she came up with naught. Major Edgewell kept his work and home separate. There was a supply of stationery, pens, and pencils. The folders in the bottom drawer contained the house ledgers and little else. No battle plans, no troop movements, and not even a requisition for supplies lay in the mix.

Dora cast a glance at the shelves. There were dozens of books. It would take far more time than she had to search them for clues. She filed them away as a last resort and exited the room.

Her sock feet made no sound as she tiptoed toward the front of the house. She ignored the dining room and went through the open door of the parlour. Here, the curtains were drawn, casting the room in a shroud of darkness. Dora closed the door, cursing when the hinge squeaked. She froze, but heard no indication that anyone above had taken notice.

She forced air into her lungs and slid the candle stub from her pocket. She'd come prepared with a light source and matches for the flame.

Dora moved as quickly as the flame of her candle would allow. The basket of knitting was exactly where she'd last seen it. She committed the order of the objects to memory, taking them out and putting them back in after a fruitless search. Nothing hidden there except a pair of spectacles.

Dora leaned over and ran her hand between the cushion and the armrest of the chair where Theresa had sat. All she felt was the smooth surface of the upholstery. She dug deeper, checking whether the bible might have fallen into the gap.

"Where's the word of the Lord when you really need it?" she muttered. Her eyes turned to the desk. It was still closed tight, with no key in the lock. Not that this slowed Dora. She'd picked locks of this nature hundreds of times to snoop on her mother, brothers, and sister. With a deft flick of her wrist, her metal tool coaxed the latch sideways.

Theresa's desk was a mirror image of her husband's. There was some correspondence nestled in the row of shelves. Feminine handwriting and British addresses adorned the envelopes. Nonetheless, these Dora did check one by one. All she found were boring letters sharing snippets of daily life back at home.

Try as she might, she couldn't find the bible anywhere. Theresa must have taken it upstairs with her. Dora knew she had to get her hands on it. Whatever the cost, whatever the risk, it was worth it. She had sensed half-truths and hidden secrets in her earlier conversation with Theresa Edgewell. The woman was somehow involved in the leaking of information to their enemy.

There was no help for it. Dora didn't waste time with second thoughts. She tiptoed up the stairs, carefully testing the side of each stair before putting her full weight on it. Even then, she kept a tight hold on the rail and bannister, using her arms to bear the bulk of her mass.

She stopped below the top of the stairs and lowered until she was on her hands and knees. Dora kept her head close to the carpet runner as she peered either direction of the short hall. There were four doors, two on either side of the stairs. All four were closed tight. Two were dark, and two had narrow beams of light shining under their bottoms.

Dora leaned her ear against the wall, listening carefully. There was the sound of running water and splashing.

Theresa Edgewell was busy with her nightly ablutions. Dora slipped up the remaining stairs and slowly twisted open the door on the other side of the stairs. She found a bedroom, empty, with a pale white gown lying across a ruffled spread and a man's robe draped over a rocking chair. The bible she so coveted sat on the nearest bedside table.

She grabbed it, but before she could flip open the cover, she heard the bathroom door open with a creak.

Quick as she could, she laid the bible back where she'd found it, cursing under her breath, and crawled under the bed.

There she stayed perfectly still for what felt like hours, but was only minutes. Theresa's bare feet padded around the room. Dora watched them as Theresa changed out of her skirt and blouse and into her gown. When Theresa turned off the light and dropped onto her knees beside the bed, Dora thought for sure she was caught. Instead, Theresa launched into a long-winded nightly prayer.

Theresa thanked God for her blessings and trials. Dora smiled when she heard Theresa mention her own name, with a request for guidance for the lost lamb. On and on Theresa went, finally ending with a word about her husband.

"Lord, our Father, please forgive Timothy for being late with his own prayers this evening. If you can spare the time, read the contents of his heart. There you will find the names of the men over whom he would normally ask you to keep watch. May your blessings shine upon us all for the remainder of our days. Amen."

Dora had plenty of time to ponder over those words while Theresa climbed into bed and drifted off to sleep. Long after her breathing grew regular, Dora finally crept from her hiding place. She picked up the bible and gave the binding a quick shake, with the pages facing her hand. Several scraps of paper tumbled out, landing on Dora's waiting palm.

She knew without checking that she had the proof she needed to allow Lord Audley to punish his traitor.

Chapter 13

The Cat Chases The Mouse

Rex rolled up his shirtsleeves, wishing for even a tiny draft of the cool night air to offset the cloying stillness. Sitting deep within the warehouse, he was far from any door or window. Even his imagination struggled to conjure up any sense of a breeze.

He'd left his sling at home, and his injured arm was busy protesting that decision. He rested his elbow on the edge of a nearby crate and tuned out the dull flame of pain. Rex had a purpose for being in the warehouse long after normal working hours. He'd eaten dinner and taken care of his needs before entering through a rear door using a key Lord Audley had provided.

He wasn't staking out the warehouse at random. After he'd combed through the paperwork, Rex had spotted a pattern everyone else had overlooked. The thefts generally occurred on the same night as the senior officer's card game. They had invited Rex enough times for him to know when it happened. The dates fluctuated depending on who was available and ongoing missions. Only someone aware of the event could have made the connection.

That wasn't the only thing that caught Rex's eye. It wasn't so much when the card games happened as who attended them. Major Edgewell was a regular, although he had a reputation for bowing out early. How many times had they ribbed the Major for wanting to get home to his wife? Rex had never considered that the man might be up to something else.

Now, he had to see for himself. Thus, why he was hiding in a dark warehouse, late at night. The church bells had rung the eleventh hour. Rex fought the urge to yawn and decided he'd better move around before he fell asleep. He could afford to move around. The warehouse maze offered no shortage of hiding places. The moonlight was fighting a losing battle against the dust and salt coating the skylight.

During his third circle around the back half of the storage area, Rex heard a rattling coming from behind. It was the rear door, the same one he'd used to come inside. He'd taken care to lock the door behind him. Had that been a mistake?

The click of the lock turning over answered that question. Far too little time had passed for someone to have picked it. The person coming in had a key, just like he did.

Rex slid soundlessly along the aisle, taking care to keep to the shadows. A man strode through the door, walking confidently into the warehouse, as though he had every right to be there. He carried a pail in his hand.

Although Rex couldn't see his face, he knew this wasn't the case. The real guard had passed through ten minutes earlier and wasn't due to make another check until after midnight.

Despite his confidence that this was the intruder, Rex held back on confronting the man. He needed evidence of the man's treachery.

Rex remained in the shadows, stalking the intruder as he wound through the aisles between the stacks of crates. Whoever he was, he knew his way around. Guided only by a small torch, the man passed the crates of bullets and uniforms, making his way over to where the food stuffs were stored.

The intruder grabbed a pry bar from the wall and advanced on a crate labelled as holding flour. With little care for the noise he was making, the shadowy figure wedged the flat end under the lid, and tugged on the pry bar until the nails gave way. Then he took his pail and poured liquid on the contents of the crate, turning the precious flour into sludge.

Rex acted.

"Stop! You're under arrest!" he shouted, launching toward the intruder.

The intruder spun around, saw Rex advancing on him, and launched the pail at his head. Rex was forced to duck, providing the intruder with a few seconds of advantage.

Rex leapt over the metal pail, still shouting, as he gave chase. The dirty skylights had been to Rex's advantage when he'd been in hiding. Now they worked against him. Rex couldn't go nearly as fast as the intruder, who was still holding the torch. The beam of light jerked up and down, lurching worse than a sailor on shore leave.

The rear door slammed behind the intruder. Rex burst through it in time to see the back of the man running up the alley. He was headed for the main road. Rex had to catch him before he reached it. There were too many shadowed storefronts where the mystery man could hide. Rex might run right past him without even realising it.

Rex dug deep, dredging the last of his energy stores. He cursed the fever that had zapped his stamina and cursed himself for failing to notice until now. Rex's entire focus was on closing the distance between them.

Rex nearly cheered with joy when the intruder paused at the entrance to the alley. Standing under a lamp, his uniform and cap were plain as day. British khaki, with no adornments, ubiquitous in a military town such as this one. Rex committed to memory what little he could see of the man's features.

The intruder took off again, running across the main street.

Rex chased after the villain without a thought. His feet hit the cobblestone street. He heard the blare of a horn and an angry shout. Bright spotlights blinded Rex's night vision. He threw a hand up and leapt out of the way before an oncoming car ploughed into him. The vehicle shot past, narrowly missing him.

Rex rolled across the cobblestones, his arm bursting into agony when it hit upon the solid ground. His physical pain was nothing compared to his despair. Not only had he failed to catch the intruder, Rex had barely seen enough of the man to pick him out in an identity parade.

The street was empty of any other signs of life. There was no one there to help Rex back to his feet, or to see the blood stain blossoming on his upper arm. Although he could have used the help, he was glad he was alone. There was no one to shout at him for his colossal mistake. His best chance for catching the traitor red-handed was gone.

Chapter 14
A Question Worth Considering

Dora heard the blare of the car horn and glanced around. It had been faint, likely from the next street over. It was an apt reminder that she wasn't the only one on the move after dark. She tugged the brim of her cap, further shadowing her face, and sped her steps. Staring at her feet, Dora failed to see the man coming around the corner until he smacked into her.

The man slowed long enough to call a gruff apology. Dora waved him off, somehow remembering in time to lower her voice when she grunted, "No worries."

She counted her blessings that the man had stalled no longer. She'd recognised him as Sergeant Broadmore, Major Edgewell's valet. One wrong word from him, and her cover would have been blown.

Dora passed no one else before she spotted the gate to Lord Audley's garden. This time, the study lights were still on, creating a soft glow around the edge of the drapes. The light made it easy for Dora to spot a gap in the curtains. She crept close, peering inside until she was confident only one man was in the room. Then she tapped on the glass of the door.

The curtain swished aside and Lord Audley glared out at her. She motioned for him to unlock the door and let her inside.

"You're making a habit of breaking and entering, Viscountess," Audley said, opening the door wide enough for her to join him in his study.

"I resent that. Nothing's broken, at least not so far. As for the entering, I can hardly swan in through the front door at midnight without raising eyebrows. Neither of us wants that."

"That's true. Tell me, are you here for a reason, or is this a social call?"

"I thought you might like the identity of your traitor... or one of the traitors would be more apt. If you're busy, I can come back." Dora feinted for the door, but Audley shut it before she could reach it.

"Colour me intrigued. Take a seat and tell me what you know."

Dora plopped into the nearest armchair and fanned her face, revelling in the freedom of trousers. She ignored the second part of Lord Audley's order. Before she told her what she'd found, she wanted the answer to a question of her own. The trick would be convincing him to reveal it. She'd have to force his hand.

"Your leak is Major Edgewell."

Lord Audley frowned at her from his seat. "That is highly unlikely. The man has no reason to love our enemy."

"Be that as it may, it is the truth. He may not care for the Germans, but he has a weakness they can exploit. He said it himself here the other night. His brother-in-law is in their clutches." Dora met Audley's gaze head on. "Why are you so certain of his innocence?"

Audley glanced to the side, and for a moment, Dora thought he'd lie to her. But he didn't appear to be coming up with a half-truth or other vagary. If anything, he was wrestling with his conscience. Dora would have sworn the man didn't have one.

"I tell you this only so that you can exclude Major Edgewell from consideration, and get on with ferreting out the correct answer. Edgewell's brother-in-law is not a prisoner of war. Or, I should say, he isn't anymore. The man is dead."

"Dead?" Dora reared back as though she'd been slapped. Of all things he could have said, that was the last thing she'd expected. "But at your home..."

"Yes, yes," Audley said, interrupting her. "I told Edgewell it was a terrible idea, but he insisted we keep the information from everyone, but especially his wife, until we have formal confirmation. You see, we found out through an informal source, as you might call it. The Germans have denied it, but our source was adamant that Edgewell's relative died from sepsis following a wound taken in battle."

Dora parsed the information. "You think they're keeping the truth from you because we have several of their soldiers in our ward. They fear we'll exact retribution."

Audley nodded his head, impressed she'd connected the dots so quickly. "The Edgewells have no children. Mrs Edgewell raised her brother after their parents died in a carriage accident. The major worried the news of his death will deal her a blow from which she won't recover. Given she is overseeing our team of nurses, I agreed to remain mum. I count on you to do the same."

Dora waved aside the question, murmuring assurances of her own. She wouldn't tell Theresa, but the secret was going to have to come out one way or another.

"If there's nothing else, you can leave the same way you came in," Audley said, rising to fix himself a nightcap.

Dora didn't move from where she was sitting. "You might as

well pour two glasses, Lord Audley. I'm far from done. You didn't give me a chance to finish."

For once, Dora caught Audley off guard. He looked at her anew with curiosity weighing his brows. He took a second glass from his shelf and splashed a finger of scotch into it before passing it to her. After she thanked him, he returned to his seat and gave her his full attention.

Dora sipped the fine liquor, tasting the hint of smoke and vanilla. It was much finer than anything she had access to in her lodgings. It was a shame she couldn't sit there longer and enjoy the experience. She spoke before Audley lost his patience.

"Major Edgewell is your leak," she said, raising a finger. "However, I would bet my dowry he has no idea. He isn't sharing inside information willingly, Lord Audley. His problem is that he is unaware someone else is listening."

"Go on," Audley said, well and truly intrigued.

"You'd have to be blind, deaf, and dumb to overlook his family's religious fervour. While it might give them an inner strength, it is also their weakness. Every night, before going to sleep, the major puts in a good word with God for the men heading off into the field. Your traitor is eavesdropping on his conversations with the man above and feeding those details to the other side."

"My god!" Audley blurted before he realised the irony of his statement. "Who is eavesdropping, and how did you figure this out? I assume you have proof."

"I do," Dora answered, patting her pocket. "Sit back, sip your drink, and I'll tell you the entire story."

Dora told Lord Audley about her visit to Theresa Edgewell, and her request for aid in resolving her inner turmoil. "Theresa is ever eager to spout off a bible reference, but when she wants to make a specific point, she always opens the good book and reads the exact verse. It struck me as odd that she had this particular verse memorised, and that she was unwilling to turn to that page in front of me."

"What verse was it?"

Dora answered Audley's question and then continued, "I bade her goodnight, went back to my room, and changed into this. I knew the major was off playing cards, so I took the chance to sneak in to see what she was hiding in her prized possession. At first, it seemed incredibly poor luck that Theresa had carried the bible upstairs with her. She nearly caught me in her bedroom, and I had to hide under the bed. However, divine intervention must have been at work, because I was perfectly positioned to hear her nightly prayer. I took these from her bible after she fell asleep." Dora handed Lord Audley the two slips of paper she'd taken from the house.

Audley unfolded them, reading them in silence. The messages were short and left little room for confusion.

We need more or your brother's life is forfeit. We await your next message in our usual hiding spot.

"Where is the hiding spot?" Audley asked. "Any ideas of who is retrieving the messages?"

"It has to be on the house grounds. The only other place Theresa goes with any regularity is the hospital. With as many of us as there are moving around, she'd never get away with hiding secret messages there."

Lord Audley could hardly believe what Dora was saying. His dumbfounded expression made that much clear. "Are you telling me that not only is Major Edgewell feeding secret info to the Germans via his wife, but he has somehow overlooked a stranger sneaking around on his property? Presumably multiple times!"

"He has no one to blame but himself for his blind eye. His wife boldly stated that family is more important than anything else. In pandering to her feelings, Major Edgewell left his broadside exposed for an enemy attack. "

"Indeed, Viscountess. I must say, I am impressed by your work, and more critically, with the speed at which you undertook it. You did this all yourself?"

"For the most part," Dora said. She set her mouth in a firm line, making it clear she'd keep her secrets to herself.

"This is more than sufficient to convince me of your usefulness. I will telegram your father tomorrow to let him know we need here you for the time being."

Dora finished the last of her scotch and prepared to leave.

"Before you go, I'd like to ask you a question. Call it a curiosity, if you will. If you were in my shoes, what would you do about Theresa Edgewell?"

That was a question Dora hadn't allowed herself to contemplate. She knew it would be all too easy to veer into the realm of an eye for an eye and a tooth for a tooth. She had avoided getting a taste for blood during the first of twenty years of her life, and she had no intention of succumbing to the temptation now.

Although it was very difficult to resist.

There would never be another man in this world like Lucien. She'd grown fond of him simply by listening to his sister recount tales of their childhood. Befriending him here, in Le Touquet, wasn't part of any machination. He'd understood intrinsically what it meant to be different from everyone around you and had shared her desire to live outside the confines of society. She may have threatened to out him if he didn't marry her, but only because she knew he needed a twist of the arm to agree. Once he'd got his head around what she meant, he'd been more than happy to become a coconspirator.

Theresa Edgewell had sacrificed his life to save her brother. It was not right. But some part of Dora understood her logic, flawed as it was. Sending Theresa Edgewell to the firing line wasn't going to bring him back.

That didn't mean it would be right to let her off scot-free. The mere thought of it made Dora's stomach turn. This was not a question with a quick answer.

"You ask a tough question, one that deserves proper consideration. If it is acceptable, I will return tomorrow night, after the sun sets, with my reply."

Lord Audley agreed, gazing upon her with a newfound respect as he showed her out the rear door.

Dora tossed and turned again that night. She awoke with a fierce headache and hair-trigger temper. Inga wisely kept at a safe distance until they arrived at the hospital ward for their early morning shift.

Dora hid in the supply cupboard and channelled her frustration into the piles of unfolded bed linens while turning the problem over in her head. What to do with Theresa? She couldn't let the woman carry on, that much was for sure. But outing her to everyone would leave both Major Edgewell and Lord Audley open for ridicule. How could they have missed such a thing taking place right under their nose?

There was only one solution. She had to figure out who was sending the messages to Theresa.

Dora replayed her conversation with Lord Audley again. He had made a good point. Major Edgewell would hardly suspect his own wife, but surely someone in their household would spot a stranger sneaking around. She'd seen herself how easy it was to bump into the wrong person. The Major's valet, Sergeant Broadmore, had nearly unmasked her the night before.

She ran out of sheets to fold. It was time to walk the ward. Maybe talking to the men would jog her memory. Dora walked into the hallway and heard a man's voice coming from the room next door.

She knew that voice. Lord Rex was here.

Dora quickly backtracked into the supply cupboard and grabbed a glass bottle from the shelf. She climbed on a stepladder, placed the bottle against the wall, and listened.

"How did you reopen your wound?" she heard the doctor say. "And more importantly, why didn't you come for help last night? You're black and blue!"

"I saw someone sneaking out of the supply hub and gave chase. I barely avoided being struck by a car as thanks for my troubles. A few scrapes and bruises weren't justification enough to give up. I spent half the night searching for any sign of the bugger. Save the lecture, I feel bad enough about losing the culprit."

"Did you at least get a look at him?"

"I did, albeit a brief one. It may take me a long while to put a name with the face, but I won't stop looking until I track him down. Whoever he is."

Dora straightened up and removed the bottle from the wall. She'd heard the squeal of tyres, and shortly after, Sergeant Broadmore had run smack into her. It could be a coincidence...

Dora made a rapid assessment of her options. Pointing Rex is the man's direction would be the fastest way to test her suspicions. If she was right, Rex would take the information to Audley and the full case would reach a natural conclusion.

All Rex needed was a nudge in the right direction.

An anonymous note left in his room—that should do the trick. She'd get Inga to cover her for half an hour and sneak it in when he was eating lunch.

Chapter 15
Justice For One

Mews was waiting on Rex's bed when he came into his room. The kitten was straddling something white and chewing on the end of it.

"What have you got there, boy?" Rex asked. He scooped the kitten up and tucked it against his chest, freeing the paper that had been underneath. It was a note, addressed to him, in an unfamiliar handwriting.

Rex wasn't expecting anything. He set the paper aside, shifted the cat to the floor, and dangled a shoelace in front of it. The cat now suitably distracted, Rex unfolded the note and skimmed the contents.

I overheard you in the hospital. Sergeant Broadmore knocked me down while running away from you. He is a menace to society. Since you're a captain, maybe you'll have better luck doing something about it.

Rex flipped the paper over and examined the outside more closely. There were no distinguishing marks, and the size and shape matched the pads he'd seen the medical officers using.

He didn't know whether to dare to trust the contents. He

was far too skeptical to believe clues fell like manna from heaven.

But then again, what did he have to lose?

It wasn't as though he had a better idea of where to begin. Trotting back to Audley's office with his tail between his legs was equally unpalatable.

Lucky for him, his afternoon was free of obligations. A discreet word with a friend and he'd figure out who this Broadmore was in no time and where to find him. He headed over to the housing office, where he could strike two birds with one stone. His old school chum Clark Kenworthy sat at the desk.

"Clark, old boy, you're just the man I hoped to see."

"Need to win some money back?" Clark replied, spearing Rex with an uncompromising gaze. "I learnt my lesson at Eton, so count me out of your gambling schemes."

Rex pretended to stagger. "You wound me, and as you can see, I'm already injured. Lucky for me, it's information I'm after and not your purse. I'm looking for a Sergeant Broadmore. Any ideas where I might run him to ground?"

"Broadmore?" Clark repeated, cocking an eyebrow. "I'm surprised you don't know him. He's Major Edgewell's man."

Rex goggled, once again unable to believe his change in fortune. An hour ago, he'd had no idea where to look for their traitor. Now, he not only had a name, but that name was directly connected to his prime suspect. "I owe you a drink, mate!"

"You owe me two, if the elation on your face is any sign. I'll remind you the next time I bump into you at the pub."

Rex left the building, debating his next move. Although he'd made progress, his evidence was still circumstantial. He was in desperate need of hard proof of Broadmore's guilt, especially since he still didn't know whether Edgewell was involved. The more leverage he could gain over Broadmore, the better. If the man knew they had him dead to rights, he'd be more likely to blow the whistle on any associates in exchange for avoiding the noose.

Rex checked his watch. It was early afternoon. Major Edgewell and his soldier-servant would be hard at work in his office at the Hotel de Ville. Mrs Edgewell was likely making rounds at the hospital. There was no time like the present to con his way into their home.

The maid answered the door, blushing mightily when she spied the handsome soldier standing on their doorstep. "The Major and the Mrs aren't at home," she stammered.

Rex grinned. "That's why I'm here. Broadmore forgot an important document in his room and asked me to run collect it. He's tied up with the Major," he added, giving her a conspiratorial wink. "He's worried about getting into trouble for being forgetful."

Poor Tilly was too flabbergasted to question why a more senior officer was running errands for a sergeant. She took one look at his sky-blue eyes and stepped aside, blushing an even deeper shade of crimson. "Top floor, on the far right," she stammered again.

Rex took the stairs two at a time, with the maid close on his heels. With her help, he had no trouble finding the right doorway.

"I'll take it from here," he instructed, his tone leaving no room for argument. "I wouldn't want to hold you up from your work." Tilly bowed and scuppered, blushing again.

The knob turned easily under his hand. The furnishings were simple, with a bed, wardrobe, desk, and washstand. Since the desk had no drawers, Rex checked the wardrobe first. He eyed the dimensions, but they matched what he expected to find. No secret hiding spots in there. A few spare shirts and trousers hung beside a winter coat.

The bed was his next destination. His hand slid under the pillow and beneath the mattress. Still nothing. The man didn't even have a letter from family back home. Rex almost pitied him. Yet, there was still the matter of the note burning a hole in Rex's own pocket. There had to be a reason his secret helper pointed him in this direction.

He scanned the room and checked the underside of the basin and desk, and the backside of the wardrobe. Still nothing. He put himself in the other man's shoes. If he were Broadmore, where would he hide things? This small room was the only private space he had.

Unless Rex had the wrong man. He reached into his pocket to retrieve the note, but paused with his hand still in mid-air.

The pockets!

Rex tugged the wardrobe doors open again and rifled through the pockets of the spare shirt and trousers. He struck gold when he got the winter coat — the one item no one would touch, not for several months, anyway. He pulled a handful of coins and several five-pound notes. His astonishment grew when he found two crisp twenty-pound notes hiding in their midst.

This was a fortune, by any standards, certainly far more than even Rex kept on hand. Rex knew with a certainty it had not come from any pay packet because they were paid in local currency, not sterling.

This would have to be enough. Rex shoved the wad of bills and coins into his pocket. He straightened the coat, closed the wardrobe doors, and left the room as he had found it. The maid was waiting at the top of the first floor stairs.

"Did you not find it?" she asked.

"Find?" Rex halted at the foot of the staircase, wondering how she could possibly have known what he was doing.

"The document he forgot," she added. "Was it not upstairs? Should you check the Major's study?"

Rex's mind caught up with her words. "It wasn't there. Do you think it would be alright if I checked downstairs?"

"You're a captain," Tilly answered, as though his rank was proof enough for her. She showed Rex to the Major's study. Rex made a rapid turn through the papers on the desk and in the drawers, pretending to check whether they were the right one. All he found were personal letters and household accounts. He grabbed a paper at random, proclaiming it the one he needed, and made a quick exit before the maid wised up.

Rex went straight to the Hotel de Ville, not stopping until he reached Sergeant Grimsby's desk outside Lord Audley's office.

"You don't have an appointment."

"I, err," Rex pulled up short. Grimsby crossed his arms, making it clear he was in no mood for fast-talking captains attempting to wheedle their way past him.

Audley's instructions had been clear. Rex was to report only to him. But that wasn't going to happen until he gave Grimsby a compelling reason to break precedent and interrupt his superior. Rex could sit here and wait for Audley to step out. However, if Broadmore returned home before that happened, and heard about a captain searching his room, the gig would be up.

For once, timeliness was more important than keeping secrets. Fortunately, Audley had also made it clear that he trusted his sergeant to keep quiet.

Rex approached Grimsby's desk, leaned over it, and whispered, "I have evidence of treason."

Those were the magic words. Grimsby held his gaze. Rex didn't blink. Without speaking, Grimsby uncrossed his arms, pushed back his chair, and got to his feet.

"Sorry about the mistake, Captain Bankes-Fernsby. I see you have an appointment, after all." Grimsby knocked on Lord Audley's door and then showed Rex in to the inner chamber.

Rex wasted no time telling Lord Audley everything, beginning with his failed attempt to catch the thief, his visit to Major Edgewell's house, and the large amount of funds he'd found in Broadmore's coat pocket.

"I hope you'll agree that this amount of money, hidden away, has a good chance of being the fruit of ill-got gains. I got a quick look at his face before he ran across the street. However, I didn't want to approach him in case he got a look at me as well. What do you want me to do next?"

Rex's leg trembled while he waited for Audley to respond. He'd been so certain he was right on his way over, but hearing the flimsy connections coming out of his mouth, now he wasn't sure. He saw smoke, but that didn't necessarily mean there was fire. Not a dangerous one, anyway.

Audley didn't answer Rex's question. He raised his voice and shouted for his sergeant instead. "Bring me Broadmore," he ordered when Grimsby opened the door. After Grimsby left, Audley told Rex to get comfortable.

Broadmore arrived within minutes, his eyes shifting between the two men in the room.

"Take a seat, Broadmore," Audley said, leaving no room for argument.

Broadmore took the chair beside Rex. He cast the man a sideways glance, but found no explanation from that quarter.

Rex studied the man's profile. It was a perfect match from what he remembered. He waited until Audley glanced his way and then gave a single nod of confirmation.

Audley turned his glare on Broadmore. "Where were you last night?"

"At the watering hole, having a drink with a few of the boys," Broadmore answered, without missing a beat.

"Hmm," Audley replied. "Did you spot your mates a round or did everyone buy their own?"

"We've hardly money to spare," Broadmore said, his face clouding with confusion.

"Oh, I think you've got plenty, Broadmore. The problem is that it is in the wrong currency. How many rounds would you say this would buy back at home, Captain?" Audley asked, turning his attention to Rex. "There's fifty-two pounds, twelve shillings here, if my addition is correct."

Broadmore's face drained of colour.

Audley carried on. "I suppose if we check the supply cupboard here, we won't find a bucket with your fingerprints on it, will we? Nor is there a key to the supply warehouse on Rue de Saint-Omer on your keyring?"

Broadmore's panicked gaze said more than any confession. Lord Audley let Broadmore squirm while he calmly retrieved a piece of paper and dashed off a note. He passed the note to Rex with instructions to take it to the Royal Military Police provost and bring someone back in short order.

By the time Rex returned, accompanied by the police officer, Lord Audley had a signed confession in hand. The officer escorted Broadmore away in cuffs to await punishment.

After their departure, Lord Audley bade Rex to remain. "I'm impressed by your work, Captain. Before I dismiss you, I have a question I'd like you to answer."

"Of course, sir."

"It regards the fate of Broadmore. Do you think he deserves the noose?"

"I do," Rex answered, honestly.

Lord Audley steepled his fingers. "Broadmore claims he acted to protect Major Edgewell. He said the enemy threatened to kill Edgewell's brother-in-law if he failed to comply. Does that change your decision?"

Rex took a moment to think, weighing Broadmore's crimes against his motivation. That he'd been placed in a precarious position was clear. But Rex knew that being an officer came with obligations and responsibilities, the highest of which was to care for the lives of the men who fought alongside them. His answer did not change.

"Broadmore should have brought the information to his superior. In this case, that was Major Edgewell. As Edgewell's closest servant, there is no reason he should have hesitated to tell him in confidence. If he had, the outcome of all of this would have been very different. And anyway," Rex added, "I doubt that is the truth. The unexplained pay contradicts his alleged altruistic motivations."

Audley's mouth dipped into a momentary frown, but shifted back into a flat expression before Rex could guess why. "You make an excellent point. I will take your advice into consideration. Unless there is something else to add, you may go, Captain. You should expect to receive a commendation in your records and your choice of assignment once you are fully healed."

The rewards were appreciated, but unnecessary. Rex knew he'd have pursued the truth without them. He'd owed it to Lucien, and to all the others Broadmore had put at risk, to uncover the reason their mission had gone so wrong. Every day they were at war, Rex depended on those around him to look out for his safety. How could he do any less?

It was that burden of responsibility that called Rex to be completely honest with Lord Audley, and to share the one part of the story he'd kept to himself.

"There's something I need to tell you, and I'll understand if you want to take back your last words."

Lord Audley cocked his head to the side and studied the man sitting on the other side of his desk. "I'm listening."

"I did as you asked. I told no one what I was doing, nor did I give any hint of it, I swear. But someone else knew. They left me a note in my room, pointing me toward Broadmore."

Audley's head straightened, and the corners of his mouth tilted upward. "A fellow officer?"

Rex shrugged. "Maybe... but I've been leaving my window open. In truth, anyone could have stuck a hand through it to leave the message on my bed. I doubt we'll ever know for certain, but I felt I should mention it."

Audley's mouth curved into a knowing smirk. "It will remain a mystery. My rewards stand. Good day, Captain. His Majesty thanks you for going above and beyond."

Chapter 16
A New Door Opens

Late in the afternoon, a thunderous rainstorm heralded the end of the extraordinary heat wave. Audley was waiting at his back garden, smoking a cigar, when Dora made her appearance after sunset. She bobbed her head in greeting and thanked him when he held open the door for her to enter his study.

They took up position in the exact same chairs they'd sat in the night before. With Dora once again dressed in her tailored uniform, one might think they'd been sitting there all night.

"I heard you arrested Broadmore," Dora said.

"Yes, Lord Rex discovered an inexplicably large sum hidden in the man's wardrobe. Under questioning, Broadmore admitted he did it for the money. It seems he intended to abscond from His Majesty's service when his turn at valet was done." Audley met Dora's eye. "Rex mentioned he'd received an anonymous note left in his room."

"Fascinating," Dora cooed, batting her lashes. "Did you know the man is keeping a kitten in his room? Bankes-Fernsby, that is. Not Broadmore."

"Indeed?" Lord Audley chuckled for the first time in a good

long while. "That explains the open window. Enough of that. Let's move on to more important topics. Have you reached a decision regarding Theresa Edgewell's future?"

"I have," Dora said. "I find it interesting that you asked me this question. The law is clear. She should be tried for war treason and judged by the courts."

"Humour me, Viscountess. Pretend you are the judge overseeing the case."

Dora knew he wouldn't let her off the hook. She'd come prepared with a response, although she wasn't sure he'd like it. "Let us be frank, Lord Audley. My pretending to be a judge is likely as close as Theresa Edgewell will come to the courts. We cannot publicly try her for her crimes without making a number of individuals look bad. For this same reason, we cannot execute her."

"You would pardon her?"

"Oh no, not by a country mile, neither her nor her husband. Major Edgewell is guilty of hubris for thinking he knew what was best for his wife without weighing the consequences. Theresa violated one of the ten commandments, the sixth to be precise. I'd sentence her to live with the knowledge of what she has done, and Major Edgewell along with her. Ship them back to England, banish them from society, and let them pray to their God for forgiveness for their sins. Although, between you and me, I don't believe even a lifetime of atonement will save them from an eternity in hell."

"No monetary fine, no hard labour?" Audley asked.

Dora shook her head. "Whose judgement and punishment can compare to that of our Lord? Let Broadmore fall on the sword for his part in the crimes."

"Wise words, indeed. I came to the same conclusion myself. The Edgewells will be on the next ship back to England. With Broadmore behind bars, that puts an end to any spying on my private conversations and brings our work together to a close. May I offer you a drink before you leave?"

"By all means." Dora relaxed in her seat, feeling the last of the burden she'd been carrying slip from her shoulders. She'd done everything she set out to accomplish. Lucien's killers would pay for their crimes, each in their own way. More important for her personally, she'd gained Lord Audley's support, and along with it, the right to make her own decisions for her imminent future.

Now that she had space to breathe freely, hopefully she'd figure out what it was that she wanted to do.

Lord Audley returned to his armchair with a glass of amber liquid in each hand. He passed one to Dora before getting comfortable. "A toast in memory of Lucien," he said, raising his glass high. Dora followed suit, a comfortable silence falling while they sipped their drinks.

Lord Audley cleared his throat to get Dora's attention. "If you are in no hurry to return home, could I ask you a hypothetical question?"

Dora waved him on.

"Would you like to *do* great acts or *be known for* doing great acts?"

Dora cocked her head to the side, her brow knitted in confusion. "I don't understand the difference. What do you mean?"

Lord Audley briefly met her gaze over the top of his glass. "Over the last few years, many men have gained recognition for their incredible feats of bravery and heroism. These men's names will be recorded in the history books and likely honoured many times over in the years to come. My question is, do you want to be one of them? Or are you satisfied with the alternative — to do great deeds under the cover of darkness, just as you have done this past week?"

Dora could not deny the appeal of having her name forever enshrined in history, known for taking risks and making sacrifices in the interest of doing what was right. How many times as a child had she read about history's infamous female rulers and wished she could be one of them?

However, there was something in Lord Audley's hooded gaze that led her to believe that wasn't the answer he sought. His question was far from hypothetical. Everything Dora suspected crystallised into a single truth.

Lord Audley oversaw far, far more than the men fighting on the Western Front. He'd as much admitted it when he spoke of learning the fate of Theresa Edgewell's brother from an informal source.

For Dora's entire life, she'd viewed the world in black and white. Her choices were stark — marry or remain dependent on her family. She'd thought herself ever so clever for finding a loophole with Lucien's help. Marrying an impossibly unsuitable man seemed the only way to buy her freedom from society.

But wasn't she free from society right now? Her parents would be aghast to see her sitting, unchaperoned after dark, with Lord Audley. The fact that she was wearing men's clothes made the situation only that much more egregiously wrong.

On the battlefield, many of the restrictions of social class had been erased. Those back in England would face an impossible task if they tried to re-institute the boundaries between men.

Dora knew the signs. The war would soon end. The arrival of the Americans all but guaranteed the allies' eventual success. There'd be peace to negotiate, but the hidden war of secrets and lies would not end when the ink dried.

The world had changed too much to ever return to the innocence of before. Men like Lord Audley would use every tool available to ensure advance warning of problems looming on the horizon.

Lord Audley's question may have seemed black and white. In truth, he was shining a brief spotlight on the grey space that lay in between. He wanted to know whether Dora recognised it.

Dora felt the power shift within the room. Audley needed help. He needed her. God save her, she wanted to give it. However, if she wanted any hope of control over her destiny, she had to make him say the words.

"You speak of glory. Tell me about the alternative," she said. Her placid expression gave no hint of her thoughts.

"The history books will say it was prowess on the battlefield and management of supply lines that ensured the winner of this fight. I know differently. As you have seen this week, the outcome of the war often hinges on the acts which happen in the shadows. You've impressed me, Viscountess, and that isn't easy to do. I am offering you an opportunity to do more of what you've shown you can do best. I'm trusting that you will keep this information to yourself should you choose not to take me up on it."

Dora stilled. Her future pathway, so carefully mapped, trembled.

"I am in need of people who can pass behind enemy lines. Specifically, I need someone who can move within the upper echelons of society, gathering information on the decision-makers and those who whisper in their ears. I think you could be one such individual. You have the training and the education to pull it off without ever arousing suspicion."

Dorothy sat up straighter. "The Viscountess of Lisle can go many places, but to act as a spy behind enemy lines?" She laughed. "They'd never let me past the border, more or less into the upper echelons of society."

Lord Audley's smile took on a decidedly evil bent. "The

Viscountess cannot go to these places. If you were to choose to undertake this task, the Viscountess would have to retire to the countryside to live a life of permanent mourning over the loss of her husband so soon after their wedding day."

"I'm not sure anyone who knows me would believe that..." she murmured.

"War has wrought changes less strange, I assure you," he countered. "You, my dear girl, have the chance to be re-birthed. You would take on a new identity and carve for yourself a future independent of anything and anyone you know right now. I warn you, however, it will not be easy. You would have to say goodbye to everyone that you know and love."

"What of my parents?" Dora asked, suddenly balking at the choice that had seemed so easy until that moment. "They've lost one child. You cannot mean to deprive them completely of another. It won't be as though they can pop out to the countryside for a visit. I'll hardly be there."

"Err, yes," Audley's constant confidence wobbled.

"You could tell them. You, not anyone else," Dora added, pressing her moment of advantage. "Tell my father and let him break the news to my mother. He won't approve, I'm sure, but he will understand. I've been headstrong since the day I was born, or so he says."

Audley shifted in his chair, but could find no counter-argument to her proposal. "Fine, but it may be some time before I can travel back to England."

"Excellent," Dora said, feeling once again in control. "Shall we return to your question? You spoke hypothetically, but surely actions speak louder than words. I could have come to you this morning with the information about Broadmore. Instead, I chose to get word to Lord Rex. Yes, he was in a better position with regard to evidence in hand, but that wasn't the only thing guiding my hand."

"Why did you tell Rex about Broadmore?"

"Deep inside, I knew that Rex and I shared the same drive to see vengeance for Lucien's death. Catching Theresa brought me closure. Rex deserved the same. That it would make your life easier was little more than a bonus."

Audley barked a laugh at her audacity.

"You know what my answer is, Audley. I will join your corps. You will find a way to get word to my parents. The DeVere family has a house in Provence. Lucien's sister is my dearest friend. I can count on her to maintain my cover story. I'll put everything in place and you can send word of my first assignment."

"I... what?" Audley spluttered.

"I'll need to find someone who looks enough like me to play the role of the grieving viscountess. Lucky for us both, no one has seen me in years. The war delayed my debut. I can use the time to develop my cover story. I'll also have need of a companion I can trust. No woman of the upper class would travel entirely on her own."

Lord Audley sighed. He'd somehow gone from having the upper hand to being on the back foot. For the first time, he understood exactly why young Lady Dorothy Cavendish had caused her father's hair to turn prematurely grey.

"I take it you have someone in mind."

Dora knocked back her drink and rose to her feet. "I know just the dame for the job. You'll like her, Lord Audley. Even better, her first name is of Germanic origin."

Lord Audley resisted the urge to cover his face with his hands. "Fine, fine. I trust your choice in the matter. Before you dash off, I'll offer a last piece of advice. Choose a cover name that will be easy for you to remember. A middle name or something similar."

Dora grinned when the perfect name came to mind. "I'll

borrow a name from the most powerful woman in ancient Byzantine and use one of Lucien's given names as a surname."

Lord Audley arched his eyebrows in a silent question.

Dora struck a pose, positioning herself so the light highlighted her best features. "From today onwards, you may call me Theodora Laurent."

* * *

Do you want to read more Dora and Rex Mysteries? You're in luck! Their adventures continue in **Murder, I Spy**.

Set in the glittering ballrooms of 1920s London, Dora and Rex have to work together to uncover the identity of a cold-blooded killer.

Dora, however, has one minor problem. As far as the world is concerned, she's Theodora Laurent, femme fatale of the social scene. She and Rex must solve the case before her real identity comes out. She doesn't dare trust anyone with her secret — not even Lord Rex!

You can grab Murder, I Spy right now on Amazon.

Read on for an excerpt.....

Murder, I Spy

London, 1922 - Dora and Rex finally come face-to-face when they have to work together to solve the murder of a shared connection. Want a sneak peek?

* * *

Chapter One from Murder, I Spy

The complete upheaval of Lord Reginald's future started the moment he crumpled his newspaper into a ball and tossed it into the terrine of hot porridge sitting in the middle of the dining table.

The dining room of this particular home had seen its fair share of temper tantrums over the years, despite being a study in elegance and simplicity. The walls were painted in a pale sage and the curtains pulled back to let in an abundance of sunlight. High-backed chairs upholstered in cream silk surrounded a long, rectangular table made of oak. Located just off Grosvenor Square in Mayfair, the behaviour of the occupants proved that an excellent address and rich furnishings weren't enough to enforce a stiff upper lip.

That didn't mean, however, that its current owner, the Dowager Duchess of Rockingham, welcomed such behaviour. She was a doyenne of the upper class, known as much for her immaculate style as her encyclopaedic knowledge of England's elite. She much preferred to capture titillating snippets of gossip through her intricate web of informants than witness it from a member of her own family.

When the aforementioned broadsheet landed with a splat, sending a glop of porridge onto her starched white linen tablecloth, she was less than pleased. She arched an eyebrow at the fair-haired man seated across from her while the footman rushed to remove the offending object.

"Was the news not to your liking, dear, or was it the porridge? If you want extra seasoning, you need only to send word to Cook."

Lord Reginald, known to friends and family more simply as Rex, flushed in embarrassment. He'd been so engrossed in the paper, he'd quite forgotten his grandmother was still sitting at the table.

"Apologies, Grandmama. There's nothing wrong with the food." Rex speared a bite of egg with his fork to emphasise his point. "It's this situation with Freddie that's causing me indigestion."

His grandmother's expression softened, the disapproval replaced by genuine sympathy. She rested a hand against the stiff lace of her bodice. "Terrible loss, that is. As if your generation didn't suffer enough death during the Great War. To lose a man such as Frederick Ponsonby to a senseless back alley murder... I still can't imagine what he was doing in such a forsaken place."

"It seems imagination is all we have left. According to the

Times, the Yard has run out of leads. They've stamped his file as *death by misadventure, caused by person(s) unknown* and seem content to leave it at that."

The Dowager Duchess shook her silvered head, the diamonds in her hair glittering under the dining room chandelier. "Poor Freddie. He deserved better, although I can't imagine the chief investigator took such a decision rashly. The Ponsonby name is well-regarded, even if the death tax left their coffers dry. I had every faith that Freddie would eventually marry an heiress and resolve the problem."

Rex was less convinced on that front, but otherwise shared his grandmother's disappointment. Freddie had been a good man, one of the best he'd known.

Although Freddie had a reputation for driving fast cars, betting on winning horses, and escorting women with questionable moral codes, Rex saw through to the real truth of his character. Freddie preferred to keep his good deeds out of sight. He'd give you the shirt off his back, and was the first to stand at your side in a challenge. While such efforts guaranteed fast friendships, they did little to rebuild a lost fortune.

Now, he was gone, found dead in the shadows of the Ten Bells, a pub in Spitalfields, with a gunshot through his heart. In an area so packed with people that they lived five or more to a room, somehow no one heard the firing of a gun. It wasn't until the morning after that someone contacted the police, and only then to request they collect the body.

Rex had used his family name to demand access to the investigation files, thin as they were. His daily trips to Scotland Yard yielded little result. It didn't matter what he said. The chief investigator had already decided Freddie's public image was as deep as Freddie got.

He'd poked his finger into Rex's chest and leaned close enough for Rex to smell the onions on his breath. "You lordlings should know better than to venture into the slums. No amount of money will guarantee your protection. Frederick Ponsonby should have kept his wagers to those within his own social class, instead of visiting that pub. Mind you, don't make the same mistake, boy."

Rex's cheeks burned hot as fury stole the words from his mouth. He'd grabbed his coat and swept from the man's office without a backward glance.

Even now, several days later, seated at his grandmother's dining table, the memory galled him.

After the footman poured the dowager a fresh cup of tea, she settled her gaze on her grandson. He was a handsome man, with sharp, angular features and a tall, lean frame. His hair was a pale blond, swept back in a stylish pompadour, and his piercing blue eyes were framed by long, dark lashes. His complexion was wan despite the first blush of a tan, marred by dark circles under his blue eyes. Had he lost weight? She recalled all the meals he'd missed in the last week. She'd thought he was at his club, but now she wasn't so sure.

Man or not, he needed a firm hand to get his life back on track. "I'm sorry to see this terrible tragedy end in such a manner, but at least you can turn your attention to other matters now."

Rex stared, unblinking. "What other matters could be more important than this, Grandmama? My friend is dead. I have no intention of letting the investigation die as well. Not so soon, anyway. There's no way they ran down every lead in such a short time."

His grandmother was unmoved. In a voice as steely as her rigid spine, she replied, "It is done, Rex. Accept his death and mourn him, but your attempts to manoeuvre the team at Scotland Yard are at an end. This level of involvement is unhealthy... Particularly for you." She tilted her head so her stately profile caught the sunlight. "I heard you cry out in your sleep last night. Again. That's the fourth time since you learned of Freddie's death."

"Fifth," Rex whispered, unable to keep the word from slipping from his lips.

"Worse than I feared. I'll ask the doctor to send over a sleeping draught. You will return to your studies. That calmed you before. Take your mind off things." She prattled on as though she were discussing a child and not a man in his mid-twenties.

Rex watched as his grandmother took his future in a firm grip, running ahead with her plans to help him deal once again with the terrors that ruined his sleep. Dreams of battlefields, of narrow escapes. In his mind's eye, the chaos of war shrank until all he saw was a severed limb beside a lifeless body. Worse yet were the nights he dreamt of the living. How many times had he revisited the final moments of those gunned down before his very eyes?

His grandmother was right in one way. He was smart enough to recognise that the only thing that would stave off the horrors in his mind was driving himself to distraction. The Chief Inspector sneered at the inane pastimes of the titled and wealthy, blind to their reasons.

He'd had only to ask the question. Why did young men like Rex and Freddie waste the hours of their days with gambling, drink, women, and dancing?

They were all too aware of just how brief life could be. They knew that there was no explanation or justification for who lived and who died. The unbearable burden of surviving weighed so heavily on Rex's shoulders that his chest grew tight and he heard his heart pounding in his head.

Yet, around the start of spring, something in Freddie had changed. His eyes grew less shadowed, and his laugh less forced.

"What's your secret?" Rex had asked. "Is it a woman? Has the great Freddie Ponsonby fallen to Cupid's bow?"

"Not likely," Freddie had said with a chuckle. "I simply recognised that I'd spent far too long laying amongst the flowers. It was time for me to stand up and be a man."

Rex had scrunched his brow, not understanding what Freddie meant.

Freddie had clapped him on the shoulder, taking pity on his friend's obvious confusion. "I spent days thinking about those we lost, wondering why me and not them. For a long while, it was more weight than I could bear. But I see now that was wrong. My mourning is done. I decided to live for those who didn't."

"You've revelled in bacchanalia enough for three men," Rex agreed.

Freddie barked a laugh, but his face grew sober. "I must bring balance to my ways. I must be the brother, father, and son. Even if my universe is no larger than the confines of this city, there are still gaps I can fill. I will do what I can, and it will bring me peace."

Their friend Clark had intervened at that point, drawing Freddie away to play the latest parlour game. Rex was left to wonder in what ways Freddie intended to change. He'd longed to ask, but never again found the opportune moment.

Now, he'd never have the chance. Rex knew the truth of what happened in that back alley lay in that very question. Freddie must have been there for a reason. What gap had he seen? Who had he been helping?

Rex's grandmother demanded Rex put those questions aside, but her ask was impossible. Rex had to know. Not just for Freddie.

For himself.

Perhaps the answer would bring meaning to his life as well.

He'd never find out unless he pursued the truth of Freddie's death.

His face hardened into the steely mask he'd perfected on the front lines and he turned his gaze on the woman seated across the table.

The dowager gasped at his transformation.

"I'm no longer a child in leading strings. I will pursue this matter until the bitter end. After all," he added, chuckling darkly, "what are a few nights of lost sleep compared to eternal rest? Do not ask me again to abandon this task."

Her lips flattened into a hard line, but she nodded her agreement.

Rex made quick work of taking his leave from the table and hurrying up the grand staircase to his bedroom suite. His valet was still inside the bedchamber, brushing out the coat Rex had worn the night before.

"Did you need something, sir?" he asked, rising to his feet.

Rex waved at the slender man to keep his seat. "I would never presume to pry into your private life, Brantley, but I'm curious whether you are familiar with anyone in the Ponsonby household."

Brantley paused, brush in hand. "I can't say that I am. You might ask Cook. She has her fingers in a number of pies, if you get my drift."

Rex nodded and turned on his heels to do just that. A wayward thought stopped him in his tracks. He was assuming Freddie's valet might be aware of something because he often confided in Brantley. That kind of narrow thinking was likely why the official investigation came up dry.

"Can I ask you another question? Purely hypothetical," he added.

Brantley set the brush aside and straightened in his chair, giving Lord Rex his full attention.

"If a man were going to choose one person in whom to confide, whom might that be?"

Brantley's shoulders relaxed. "That's easy. He'd tell his wife."

"What if he didn't have a wife?"

"Does he have a woman at all? Anyone he's committed to? If not, I suppose it would be a friend or someone else he trusted. If it's a man of your class you mean, you'd know better than I who else should go on the list."

"Thank you, Brantley. As always, I value your honesty and plain speaking. For a man of my class, as you say, such gems are rare."

Brantley smiled at the compliment. "Is that why you asked me about Ponsonby's household? Are you trying to figure out what happened to him? If so, you might try knocking on the door of his lady friend first. Even if she doesn't know anything, if her photos in the paper are any sign, spending time with her wouldn't exactly be a hardship."

Rex racked his brain but came up short. He paid little attention to the ever-changing rota of women currying favour with their group. "Do you remember her name?"

"I'd be hard-pressed to forget it. Sounds like one of those French film stars. It's Theodora. Theodora Laurent, to be precise. She arrived in London six weeks ago and has been centre stage in many a man's dreams ever since."

* * *

Want to keep reading? Grab Murder, I Spy right now on Amazon.

Murder, I Spy

A Dora and Rex 1920s Mystery

When a bright young man teams up with a glamorous femme fatale, the identity of a murderer won't be the only secret they'll unmask.

London, 1922. Between gallivanting in his Rolls-Royce, darkening the doorways of London's hotspots, and generally treating the Big Smoke as his playground, Lord Reginald "Rex" Bankes-Fernsby has almost succeeded in banishing the battlefield nightmares that plague his sleep. Pity he can't say the same about that nagging lack of direction in his life.

If only he were like his best friend Freddie - self-assured, suave, and up to his ears in secrets. But when Freddie is murdered, Rex doubts the verdict of death by misadventure. Was Freddie cut down while up to no good or killed in the line of duty?

Rex turns to the only person in London capable of helping him find out - Theodora Laurent, London's infamous femme fatale and Freddie's last known lover.

Theodora has a hundred reasons to let sleeping cats lie, but those disappear into the aether when Rex shows up on her doorstep and someone takes a shot at her head. Together, they're catapulted into a race for their lives, where identifying the murderer is their only hope for survival.

There's just one problem. Freddie wasn't the only one keeping secrets. If Theodora isn't careful, her cunningly constructed empire will tumble like a house of cards.

You can Get Murder, I Spy on Amazon.

Le Touquet in 1918

During WWI, the allies took advantage of the ports of northern France to ferry men and supplies to the front lines. One of the better known locations is the seaside village Le Touquet-Paris-Plage.

Officers and nurses called the hotels and houses in Le Touquet home, while enlisted men lived further up the road in the stinky, muddy tents in Étaples, France. This very obvious divide between the haves and the have-nots led to understandable disquiet among the average soldiers, and eventually boiled over in the Étaples mutiny of 1917.

When researching potential settings for this book, Le Touquet quickly rose to the top of my list, not in the least because it was easier to imagine Dora sneaking around a village than in between the tents of the front lines. With officers passing through on their way to and from the battlefields, I felt certain Dora could get away with dressing up as an officer and slinking around the shadows. The harsh line between officer and enlisted gave me the seed of an idea for who might betray Lucien and Rex.

Le Touquet in 1918

Like all fiction writers, I took some liberties with the place and time in order to craft a convincing tale. I consulted a number of websites and books for research. All mistakes are my own.

Acknowledgments

Many thanks to Ken Morrison and Anne Radcliffe for providing editorial support with this book.

Donna Rogers at DLR Cover Designs had full creative control when it came to the covers for this series and she knocked it out of the park. I am in love with her creation.

Thanks to Brenda Chapman, Monica Cobine, and Joan Newman for reading early drafts of this book and providing valuable feedback.

A shout-out to my wonderful Zoom writing friends. Our daily sprints ensure I hit my word count and remind me that I am far from alone.

Finally, a huge thank you to all my readers — I wouldn't be here without you!

About the Author

Lynn Morrison lives in Oxford, England along with her husband, two daughters and two cats. Born and raised in Mississippi, her wanderlust attitude has led her to live in California, Italy, France, the UK, and the Netherlands. Despite having rubbed shoulders with presidential candidates and members of parliament, night-clubbed in Geneva and Prague, explored Japanese temples and scrambled through Roman ruins, Lynn's real life adventures can't compete with the stories in her mind.

She is as passionate about reading as she is writing, and can almost always be found with a book in hand. You can find out more about her on her website LynnMorrisonWriter.com.

You can chat with her directly in her Facebook group - Lynn Morrison's Not a Book Club - where she talks about books, life and anything else that crosses her mind.

facebook.com/nomadmomdiary
instagram.com/nomadmomdiary
bookbub.com/authors/lynn-morrison
goodreads.com/nomadmomdiary

Also by Lynn Morrison

Dora and Rex Mysteries

Murder at the Front

Murder, I Spy

The Missing Agent

Death Undercover

The Oxford Key Mysteries

Murder at St Margaret

Burglary at Barnard

Arson at the Ashmolean

Sabotage at Somerset

The Eternal Investigator

Post Mortem at Padua

Homicide at Holly Manor

Stakes & Spells Mysteries

Stakes & Spells

Spells & Fangs

Fangs & Cauldrons

Midlife in Raven PWF

Raven's Influence

Raven's Joy

Raven's Matriarch

Raven's Storm

Wandering Witch Urban Fantasy

A Queen Only Lives Twice

Printed in Great Britain
by Amazon

42952521R00088